Body
on the
Stairs

"Thou hast seen all their vengeance
and all their imaginations against me."
Lamentations 3:60

JIM WILCOX

Other Novels by Jim Wilcox

Body in the Baptistery
Body in the Grave
Body in the Snow

Non-Fiction
How to Do Church

Publishing Coordinator – Sharon Kizziah-Holmes
Cover Design – Jaycee DeLorenzo

Paperback-Press
an imprint of A & S Publishing
A & S Holmes, Inc.

ISBN -13: 978-1-951772-87-1

ACKNOWLEDGMENTS

As always, my Lord comes first. It is He Who gives me life and peace, and whatever ability I have to write. To Him be the glory for any good thing that might come of this.

My dear and precious wife, Del, who went to Heaven after I started this book was and still is my inspiration. I look forward to seeing her again, and it won't be long.

To Del's cousin, Jerry Cooper, to the only pilot I know, I owe a debt of gratitude for his invaluable assistance in getting Gideon and Phil down safely. Read the book to see what I mean!

And my new dear friend, Sharon Kizziah-Holmes, of Paperback Books, thank you so much for making this effort come to life and reality.

ACKNOWLEDGMENTS

CHAPTER ONE

Thursday, April 9, 1:20 a.m.

HE STRUGGLED WITH the lock-pick even though the full moon gave him more light than he really wanted. *Wonder what the little shyster has against this guy. Wants him dead that's for sure.* He took a deep breath and eased the door open thankful that the high wall enclosing the back yard of the condominium hid him from the neighbors.

~~~~~

Bruno woke with a start at the sound of scratching on the back door. The big German shepherd silently made his way to the bedroom of his master. The door was intentionally left slightly ajar so Bruno could push it open with his nose. His claws scratched softly on the carpet as he made his way to the side of the bed. He put his cold, wet nose against Gideon Grant's cheek and his large paw on his
~~~~~

arm.

Grant, immediately awake, sat up on the side of the bed and placed his hand on the dog's large head. "What's goin' on, boy? You hear something?"

Without a sound Bruno turned to the door leading to the hall. When he reached the door, he stopped and looked back to see if his master was following.

He was, and in his right hand he held a fully loaded .45 caliber Sig Sauer automatic pistol which he had quietly removed from the top drawer of the nightstand. With his left-hand Grant took a firm hold on Bruno's collar. Barefoot, crouching to maintain his grip on the dog's collar, Grant softly padded out into the hall and stopped stock still to listen and watch for any movement. He whispered, "Sit, Bruno. I don't want you getting shot again."

A few months earlier, as Grant was walking a trail with his fiancé, June Whitlow, Bruno had taken an arrow tipped with a wicked Grim Reaper arrowhead that was meant for Grant.

The red spot of the laser gun sight on the intruder's weapon played on the opposite wall from where Grant stood. As the crimson dot moved across the hall toward Grant he instantly fell back into the bedroom dragging the dog with him. The silenced pistol coughed and a bullet plowed into the wall behind where Grant had been standing.

Because of his deep Christian faith in God and the consciousness of His presence Grant practiced A.S.A.P., *always say a prayer*, "Thank you, Lord, for the near miss. Help me now, please."

Grant's shoulder was almost jerked out of its socket as Bruno growled and lunged toward the door in an effort to get to the intruder. "Stay, Bruno, sit," Grant said softly. Growling and trembling, Bruno obeyed.

"Keep that mutt under control or he's dead meat," a menacing male voice said.

"You'll have to shoot me first," Grant growled in return. "You may as well know that I'm armed and I'm an ex-cop so I'm not gonna make this easy for you." He sat on the bedroom floor holding his breath and Bruno's collar listening intently for any sound that would give away the intruder's location or movement. Nothing.

The next sound he heard was the click of the latch on the back door as the intruder let himself out. Grant leaped to his feet and ran toward the front door knowing that the intruder was unlikely to try to get over the seven-foot brick and stone wall that bordered the area behind his condo. Bruno, eager to attack the intruder, ran into Grant's legs causing him to fall headlong into the entryway banging his head against the heavy front door. By the time he'd gathered himself together and opened the front door the intruder was speeding away on a quiet running Honda motorcycle.

Chance for one shot, Grant thought as he spread his legs into a shooter's stance, quickly took aim at the rear tire of the cycle and squeezed off one round. The explosion of the .45 caliber round echoed off the surrounding buildings disturbing the early morning quiet. When the tire blew the bike jerked sideways driving it into one of the brick mailbox enclosures. The rider sailed over the handlebars head long into the bricks. A sickening crack caused Grant to think, *That doesn't sound good.*

The motorcycle was still running when Grant arrived at the crash site but the intruder didn't move at all. Grant placed two fingers on the man's neck but there was no pulse. "Rats, I wanted to take him alive."

"Now, how do I shut this thing off?" Never having ridden a motorcycle it took him a moment to figure out how to turn off the engine with the key. He ran his hands through the biker's pockets looking for some identification but there was none to be found. "Professional hit-man," he said to himself. *"Now, who's mad enough at me to send a pro after me? That'd be expensive. That is if this guy's any good, which at the moment seems doubtful.*"

Lights began coming on in the surrounding condos. A couple of the more adventurous souls came out their front doors to see what had disturbed their sleep.

Grant recognized a young businessman he'd met soon after moving into the complex. "Hey, Kurt, we've got a dead man here. I got out without my cell. Would you call 911 for me?"

Kurt, a bit frazzled, stammered, "Sure…okay." He hurried back into his condo to use his land line. A couple minutes later he returned and said, "Police are on their way."

"Thanks," Grant said. Bruno strained to be free from Grant's grip on his collar. His instinct led him to believe he should take a bite out of the man who intruded into his master's house. Dead or alive, it didn't matter to him.

"Kurt, can you stay out here and watch all this for a minute? I need to go back to the house and get a leash for my dog before he pulls my arm off. And," he said looking down at his pajama bottoms and bare feet, and feeling the chill of the early morning air, "I guess I ought to get some other clothes on, too."

Kurt hesitated for a moment but said, "Okay, but hurry."

"Thanks again. Come on, Bruno, let's get back to the house." The condo, one of the more luxurious in town, was purchased by Grant a year ago with proceeds of a lawsuit brought against a trucking company in Kansas City, Kansas by the wife of his then partner. The wife, an assassin, had died while trying to kill Grant. His former partner, Roland Rounds, was serving a life term in a Texas prison for murder.

Back in his bedroom, a full-length mirror reflected his six-foot three inch, two-hundred-twenty-five-pound body. There were scars on his head and shoulder from gunshot wounds that had come close to taking his life. Hereditary baldness caused him to keep his head shaved. He recently grew a black mustache and goatee that his fiancé, June Whitlow, liked to tease him about, even though she liked it a lot. He pulled on a pair of jeans and a Missouri State University sweatshirt and slipped his feet into a pair of loafers sans socks.

~~~~~

As Gideon Grant returned to the scene, he had to shield his eyes from the bright red and blue lights on the light bars of two Springfield Police Department black and whites. Before exiting their cars the officers focused spot lights on the body of the would be killer. Warned by dispatch that at least one shot had been fired; the officers piled out of their units with their right hands resting on their weapons.

Fortunately, the older of the two officers, Corporal Lane Brooks, recognized Grant. “Hey, Gideon, didn’t know you lived in such high cotton. Still can’t stay out of trouble, huh?” He grinned at Grant and extended his hand for a friendly shake.

“Seems that way, Lane. Good to see you.”

Brooks introduced Grant to the other officer. Since he was rather new to the department he and Grant were not acquainted. “Gideon’s one of the good guys, even if he is a PI. now”

Corporal Brooks pulled a pen and pad from his pocket to take notes for his report. “Okay, what happened here?”

Grant took a deep breath and looked at his wristwatch, “Well, it seems like an hour ago, but I guess it was about twenty minutes ago, Bruno here woke me up and when I went out into the hall to see what was up…this guy put a laser spot on me. Thank the Lord he was too slow at pulling the trigger so I was able to jump back into the bedroom. He fired one round which, of course, missed; or I wouldn’t be standing here. Bruno growled and tried to get at the guy but
~~~~~

I kept hold on his collar. I told him I was armed and an ex-cop. I guess that spooked him because he went out the back door. I knew he'd have to go around to the front because of the wall out back so I ran out the front door and got off one round into the back tire of his bike. I'd hoped to take him alive since I'd really like to know why he was after me and who sent him."

Brooks continued writing for a few seconds after Grant finished. He then said, "That was a good shot. Of course, you always were one of the best shots in the SPD before…" He didn't need to finish the sentence. Grant knew he was thinking, *"Before you got kicked off the police force for too much booze and coming to work drunk."*

"I guess you'll have to take my weapon for the investigation," Grant said as he ejected the clip and the round in the chamber before handing them to Brooks.

"Yeah, 'fraid so. Shouldn't be too long, though. Seems pretty cut and dried."

As Brooks was speaking, a civilian car pulled in behind the blue and whites. Gideon's best friend and mentor, SPD Major Richard 'Dick' Jenkins got out and walked toward them. "I was at the office working on something when the call came in. You okay, Gideon?"

"By the grace of God I am. This guy," he pointed down to the deceased hit man, "broke into my place and took a shot at me. He doesn't have any ID on him so I guess you guys will have to ID him by his fingerprints. Sure would like to know who sent him…and why."

Jenkins asked, "Do either of you officers recognize this man?"

They both shook their heads and simultaneously. But Corporal Brooks said, "I can't be sure, Sir. But he does look familiar."

"Could be from out of town, Sir," the younger officer said.

"Great," muttered Jenkins, "just what we need with

everything else going on; imported trouble."

CHAPTER TWO

Thursday, April 9

GIDEON GRANT WAS at his desk in the offices of *Grant and Oppermann Investigations* by seven the next morning. Located on Battlefield Road, a high traffic street, their office was exposed to many people, which made the high lease cost worth it. Olga Oppermann, his German born partner walked into his office at 8:20 with two fresh cups of coffee. Grant was addicted to strong, black coffee and Olga was getting there.

An imposing figure at six feet and about one hundred ninety pounds, the blonde-haired PI intimidated most people who came up against her. She was one of those women who could not be called pretty but at the same time was not unattractive. No one who knew her had any doubt as to her superior intelligence.

Grant glanced at Olga briefly as she sat across from his desk and went back to his computer screen.

"What are you looking for?" she asked.

"Goin' over some old cases looking for some clue as to who would send a professional hit man after me."

"What are you talking about?" Olga was not yet in the loop about the activities of the early morning hours.

Grant turned from the computer and put is elbows on his desk. "Last night, just awhile after midnight, a man with a highly sophisticated laser equipped pistol picked the lock on my back door and entered my condo. If it hadn't been for Bruno I'd probably be dead now."

"Why did you not call me?"

As partners, Gideon and Olga, discussed every case and kept each other in the loop in every investigation.

"The place was crawling with cops within half an hour—even Dick showed up. By the time they got through with the scene and questioning me and all my neighbors it was almost five. There was no point disturbing you."

"You say that Bruno saved you? How?"

"Evidently he heard the guy and came into my bedroom and woke me up. After he took a shot at me and I hid in the bedroom, I told him I was armed and an ex-cop."

"What happened then?"

He told her the story up the time the cops finished questioning him.

"So you have no idea who he was, or who sent him?"

"Not a clue."

The phone rang and Bert Young, their secretary, answered it. They sipped their coffee and waited for her to tell them who called. "Boss, its Dick Jenkins for you."

"Thanks, Bert. Morning, Dick, what've you got?"

"Two things actually. First, you can pick up your pistol whenever you like. Since you didn't hit your shooter, Bando, with it we can release it now."

"Great, I'll come by sometime today for it. You say his name is Bando?" Grant said. "What else did you find out?"

"Perp's prints bring up an interesting story. Name's Gregory Bando. And he's not from out of town as we suspected. Lives in a trailer park on the west side of town. Rap sheet as long as your arm; two time looser—served time for extortion. A few years ago he was tried for murder twice down in Branson, but got off both times—witnesses turned up dead and evidence disappeared."

"Sounds like he was connected."

"Sure does," Jenkins said.

"What killed Bando? I wanted him alive, that's why I shot the tire on his bike."

"ME said he broke his neck when he flew into that brick mailbox. Died instantly."

"Did you find anything interesting on his bike?"

"Saddlebags had some extra clothes, a shaving kit and about $10,000 in small bills."

Grant grinned and said, "I must be valuable to someone."

"Yeah, so valuable that whoever paid Bando will probably try again."

"Just hope the next guy is as sloppy as this one."

"I wouldn't count on it. See you in church Sunday?"

Gideon Grant and Dick Jenkins were both members of Highland Baptist Church and attended as regularly as their work allowed. Jenkins, a deacon and Sunday School teacher, was the man God used to lead Grant to receive Jesus Christ as his personal Savior and Lord a few years earlier. That was back during the time when Jenkins was a lieutenant and Detective Grant was his partner in the SPD Investigations Division; before Grant's excessive drinking cost him both his job and his marriage to Diann.

He'd met Diann while they were students at MSU when he rescued her from an overzealous admirer. They had married soon after graduation and all went well until she tired of his drinking and coming late and drunk. For a long time he blamed her for the divorce which broke his heart. After becoming a Christian he acknowledged that the blame all belonged to him.

"June and I plan to be there."

"Great. Who's she prosecuting these days?"

"That man and wife team of burglars your detectives busted last year. Took this long to put a case together against them."

Jenkins said, "You should be real proud of her. The Prosecuting Attorney says she's the best Assistant PA on his team. Of course, she's the prettiest too."

"She tends to excel in everything she undertakes. That's just another reason I love her so much," Grant replied.

"You two got a wedding date nailed down yet?"

"Workin' on it. Should be soon. You and Ellen will be among the first to know. After my Mom, of course."

"Of course."

Gideon's proposal to Ardith June Whitlow happened at an elegant restaurant on the Lake of the Ozarks the previous winter. On their way back to Springfield on Interstate 44 they were attacked by two hired gunmen. June was critically wounded but with the prayers of hundreds of people and excellent care at St. Joseph's Medical Center she made a full recovery. Grant nearly lost his own life in the frigid waters of the Lake trying to take vengeance on her assailants. Convicted of his sin of seeking vengeance, he later confessed it to the Lord and promised that with the Lord's help he would never pursue it again.

CHAPTER THREE

Thursday, April 9, 4:16 p.m.

ATTORNEY MAURY SPOONER ran a one lawyer shop from a dingy second floor office in a rundown building on Commercial Street on Springfield's north side. His part-time secretary had already gone home for the day. A look at his files would reveal a very small client base, mostly small-time crooks and thugs. Even when they had money they were slow to pay for Maury's services. Maury narrowly escaped disbarment twice for alleged malfeasance in office. He spent a lot of time in local hospitals and police stations looking for clients but finding few.

Through the dirty window behind his desk the old railroad yard could be seen. Several decades ago it was the home of the Frisco Railroad. Hundreds of box cars and other freight haulers were switched there every day. Now, the trains usually just pass through. If one word was to be used to describe Maury's office, it would be *disarray*. The cheap furniture came with the office along with threadbare green carpet.

Maury picked up a copy of the Springfield News-Leader from his cluttered desk and leaned his overweight five feet, six-inch body back in his office chair. After reading several articles he came to the one he was looking for on page five. *Springfield: An investigation by detectives of the Springfield Police continues into the attempted murder of long time Springfield Private Investigator Gideon Grant. According to anonymous sources, Grant's dog alerted him to the presence of an intruder; Gregory Bando of Springfield fired one shot at Grant in his condominium and then left. Grant shot out the rear tire of Bando's motorcycle as he fled causing Bando the crash into a brick mailbox breaking his neck. He was pronounced dead at the scene.*

Maury swore as he wadded up the newspaper and tossed it at an already full trash can. The paper fell to the floor joining several Styrofoam coffee cups. "Well, Gregory, my boy, at least I don't have to worry about you spilling your guts to the cops. Tough luck for you, good luck for me. Sure would like to have the ten Gs back, it sure won't be doin' you any good."

As he pondered what to do next, he thought, *"Guess I better go see my client and see what's expected of me next."*

CHAPTER FOUR

Thursday, April 9

The offices of *Grant and Oppermann Investigations* are located on East Battlefield in Springfield, Missouri, the Queen City of the Ozarks. A large front office houses the desk and file cabinets used by the agency secretary, Alberta 'Bert' Young. Bert is married to Jimmy Young, the Assistant Chief of Police for the small city of Republic about ten miles west of Springfield. The partners' offices are in the rear of the building separated by a rear entryway, rest rooms, closet and work room. The Battlefield Road location was expensive but it provided valuable exposure to the public.

Gideon Grant took over the business when his former partner, Roland Rounds, was sent to prison in Texas for a murder committed almost three decades before. Olga Oppermann, Rounds' sister-in-law, had served Rounds and Grant Investigations as secretary for many years. Upon assuming the reigns of the business, Grant promoted Olga to detective and partner. They worked well together as equal partners but with Grant always taking the lead, which suited Olga just fine.

Olga sat in front of Grant's desk as they discussed the attack on his life. She sipped her coffee and asked, "Have you found any likely suspects in your files?"

"Too many, actually. But the most likely would probably be Marcos Deconetti and the trucking partners, George Sumtner and Scott Ireland. Then, of course, there's the lovely and wicked Bella Dubois-Barnes. She is without doubt the most vicious and vengeful of the lot. They're the ones that had the most to lose when they went to prison. And even though they're all in prison they all still have substantial financial resources at their disposal as well as plenty of connections to dirt bags to do their dirty work."

"So, what do you plan to do?"

"To begin with," he said picking up his telephone, "I'm going to contact a Taney County Deputy Sheriff Dick told me about. He was the arresting officer in the last murder case Bando skipped on. Hopefully he can give me some help connecting Bando to someone that might know what this is all about."

~~~~~

It took a few minutes to track down Deputy Tal Sloan. "Deputy Sloan, my name is Gideon Grant of Springfield…"

"Ah, yes, you're Joe Bob Round's friend. I'm surprised we haven't met before now."

Joe Bob, aka Joseph Robert Rounds, a Greene County Deputy Sheriff, is Olga Oppermann's nephew, the son of her late sister, Ingrid Rounds and her imprisoned husband, Roland Rounds.

"Yep, you would think so. Hope I didn't catch you at a bad time."

"No more than usual. What can I do for you, Mr.
~~~~~

Grant?"

"To begin with, please call me Gideon."

"Done; and I go by Tal, short for you don't want to know what. Okay?"

"Okay. Did you guys get a report on the incident in which one of your old collars took a shot at me and missed?"

"Greg Bando—yeah, we heard about it and no one around here is in the least bit grieved that he finally came to a bad end. I personally arrested him for one of the murders he walked away from. Witnesses and evidence disappeared. I still fume when I think about it."

"I'm looking for any connections that I might follow up on that might lead to whoever hired him to send me to Heaven before my allotted time."

"Most of the people he hung around with were as broke as he was most of the time, so it's doubtful any of them hired him."

Grant thought for a moment before he spoke again. "Any organized crime figures in his circle of acquaintances that you know of?"

"Naw, Bando never got that high up the ladder in the sleazy world of crime, and besides, we don't have much organized crime around here, as you surely know."

"Yeah. Thank the Lord for that. I'm just wondering about a possible connection to an old case. Well, I appreciate your trouble. Guess this is a wild goose chase."

"Hold on a minute," Tal said, "there's a lawyer—guess you could call him that—that Bando used sometime. Can't think of his name right off, but he's a shyster. Been in trouble with the bar association. Spooner, that's it. Murry, no, Maury Spooner."

Grant sat up straighter in his chair and asked, "Oh? What do you know about Mr. Spooner?"

"Don't know much for sure, but he has a reputation for being as crooked as his pal, Bando."

"What kind of people does he represent?"

"He's a real-life ambulance chaser—hangs around the ER at hospitals and the booking room at your SPD buildings. He even prowls around down here in Branson sometimes. Always looking for clients but I don't think he finds all that many."

"Oh, yeah, I think I know who you're talking about. Short, dumpy fella. Combed over hair?"

"Yeah, that's the one. He's a pest even down here."

"He tried to talk a lady into suing me last year. Her son was kidnapped and Spooner led her to believe it was my fault and she could get some money out of me or my insurance company because of it. Thankfully, she dropped it and has since become a good friend.

"Do you know if Spooner ever visits state or federal prisons looking for clients?" Grant asked.

"I wouldn't have any knowledge of that kind of activity. Why?"

"Just a hunch I'm mulling over. Okay, Tal, good to visit with you and thanks a lot for the info on the lawyer. Give me a call sometime and we'll get together for some coffee or a meal. Might even be able to catch a Baby Cardinals game."

The double A farm club of the St. Louis Cardinals played in Springfield at the beautiful new Hammonds Field.

"Hey, that sounds like a deal," Sloan said as he hung up.

CHAPTER FIVE

Thursday, April 9, 7:07 p.m.

APA ARDITH JUNE Whitlow poured over some depositions relating to a case she was prosecuting for Greene County while she waited for Grant to arrive at her apartment to take her to dinner. She smiled as she reminisced about her first contact with Grant a little over a year earlier in Kansas City during the federal trial of mobster Marcos Deconetti and June's grandfather, Attorney M. Marvin Whitlow. Whitlow represented Deconetti and his interests from before the time she was born. *I can't believe how naïve I was growing up with the Deconetti family. I thought Grandpa Marvin hung the moon and that the Deconetti's were just rich businessmen. I never dreamed they were such monsters.*

The trial resulted in both Deconetti and her grandfather being sentenced to life in the federal penitentiary system. Because his kidneys were failing, Whitlow was sent to the Medical Center for Federal Prisoners in Springfield which has the world's largest dialysis lab.

Grandpa was always sweet to me...put me through college and law school. I had no idea of his criminal activities until I went to work for the St. Louis County Prosecutor. What really breaks me heart is that he doesn't know the Lord. I'll just keep praying for him and try to talk to him about it every time I visit him. Getting transferred down here to Springfield to be near him was the best decision I ever made. I love working in the Greene County Prosecutor's office. And then, of course, there's Gideon!

She and Gideon Grant fell in love and six months ago she was delighted to accept his proposal of marriage. She still moved slowly and suffered some pain at times from a gunshot wound received the very night of his proposal.

Not yet back to her normal athletic self, she carefully got up from her chair when the doorbell to her apartment rang. She smiled in anticipation of an evening with Grant. With a look through the peep hole in the door she twisted the knob and swung the door open wide. She opened her arms wide and was enfolded in the long arms of Gideon Grant. They stood there for several moments savoring the embrace and the feel of each other. A long, tender kiss followed but it was interrupted by the ringing of his cell phone.

Begrudgingly he disengaged his right hand and reached for the phone. He punched it on speaker with one hand and placed it near his ear. "Grant here."

"Mr. Grant," a female voice said, "please hold for Senator Burkes."

"Senator Burkes? Sure."

While he waited Grant put the phone on speaker and spoke to June. "Burkes and I played football together at M.S.U. We were never close, though."

Grant and Burkes went separate ways following graduation—Grant to the Springfield Police Department and Burkes to a career as an officer in the U. S. Army. A roadside bomb in Iraq led to the amputation of both his legs at the knees ending Captain Burkes' military career. After several months' rehabilitation getting used to walking with prosthetic legs, and a job in the office of one of Missouri's congressmen, Burkes went into politics and eventually into the State Assembly in Jefferson City. Grant had worked unsuccessfully in the campaign of his opponent in Southwest Missouri.

Burkes came on the line and said, "Gideon, I hope I'm not catching you at a bad time."

"Just about to go out the door with my fiancé for dinner, but no problem. How you doin', Gardner?"

June stared at Grant with an open mouth and wide eyes at his calling the powerful senator, a state-wide mover and shaker, by his first name.

"Well, that's why I'm calling, Gideon. I need your help with something. Would it be possible for us to get together down there in the next few days? I really can't go into this matter over the phone. I'll pay your regular rate plus expenses."

Grant frowned and thought a moment. "I guess so…sure. When and where?"

"How about Monday, 2:00 p.m. at my house in Nixa. Address is in the phone book."

"Okay, Monday it is. See you then."

"That'd be great. I really appreciate this, Gideon. I've got to have someone I can trust to look into something for me. The problem is right there in Springfield so you're the first person I thought of. But I'm afraid the matter could possibly have nation-wide significance."

I can't imagine why you'd think of me, Grant thought, but he said, "I'll be glad to do whatever I can. See you Monday."

Burkes sighed and said, "That's a relief. I'll call you if there's any change in plans. It's gotta be very private."

CHAPTER SIX

Saturday, April 18

THE SMELL OF gun smoke filled the air as Milton Sorrell grunted under the weight of his large belly as he laid a 30.30 Winchester saddle gun across a bale of hay, squinted to look through the telescopic sight in the early morning light and aimed at a paper target set up about 100 yards away. He squeezed off a round, levered another into the chamber and quickly fired it followed by a third. He laid the rifle across the hay bale and moved to a scope mounted on a tripod. He closed his left eye and examined his handiwork through the powerful lenses.

"*Tight triangulation, but a little high and right. A couple clicks left and one down and it'll be just right. That ought to satisfy Morgan*," he thought. He worked at sighting weapons he repaired out behind the barn in which his gun shop was located. Painted the traditional red, the barn had long since ceased being used for farming purposes. The old hay loft was full of junk and few boxes of spare weapon parts. He owned five hundred acres of hilly land, most of which was covered by scrub oaks and cedars. Only about a hundred acres of bottom land was suitable for agricultural purposes. He used it to produce alfalfa hay.

Morgan, he thought as he reached into the chest pocket of his bib overalls for a cigarette and lit it. The very thought of Morgan Toulair sent a shiver down Sorrell's spine. Milton Sorrell was as tough as the next guy, but there was something about Toulair that was beyond toughness. There was ruthlessness, a lack of even a shred of human decency or mercy that spoke of a man with no conscience. Because of that twisted character, Toulair usually got what he was after. Few people dared to challenge him, especially those who were the least bit acquainted with him.

Sorrell looked at his wristwatch and thought, *He's due here any minute to pick up this rifle.* The thought brought beads of sweat to his forehead.

~~~~~

Sorrell sat at his work bench repairing an automatic pistol and dreading facing Toulair. The proposition Toulair had made to him sounded too good to be true, and he held to the old proverb that says, "If it sounds too good to be true, it probably is."

He hadn't bothered to put air conditioning in the barn so the doors were open to allow for ventilation. This allowed him to hear the deep rumble of the exhaust pipes on Toulair's black Humvee when he pulled onto the gravel parking area in front of the shop. He remained seated with his back to the door as he heard Toulair exit his vehicle and crunch across the gravel to the door. The last thing Sorrell wanted was for Toulair to think he was afraid of him.

Toulair stopped at the door and stood silently waiting for Sorrell to acknowledge his presence—two grown men playing a game of chicken. It was Sorrell who broke first. He turned on his chair and said, "Oh, it's you, Morgan."
~~~~~

Toulair just grunted and said nothing as he stared at Sorrell. His eyes gleamed with disdain as he looked at a man he considered to be inferior to him.

Sorrell stood and walked to the end of the shop where a rack of rifles stood. He removed Toulair's 30.30 and carried it to its owner. "Fixed and zeroed in."

"I'll do my own zeroing in, thanks," Toulair's voice dripped with sarcasm. He looked around the shop to insure they were alone and said, "I thought your buddy, Bill, was gonna be here."

"I'm afraid Bill's gettin' cold feet; said he didn't think he wanted to get involved in the deal," Sorrell said. Bill Townsend, a retired farmer and a widower, worked part time for Sorrell in his hay operation. He cut, baled and sold the hay to local cattle operations splitting the profits with Sorrell.

Toulair stared at him with cold, dead eyes that made Sorrell shiver. "In this kind of deal a man is either in or he's out—permanently."

I've got to warn Bill to stay away from Toulair, Sorrell thought, regretting the day he'd become involved with Morgan Toulair.

"You got any info on those Barrett 50-Calibers?" Toulair asked.

"Yep. Retail they run from $8,900 to $10,400 per. Wholesale they run a bit less, but anyway you go at it they're expensive. And to secure them without the necessary government paperwork runs the cost through the roof. That brings the threat of serious prison time if you're caught by ATF."

"My buyer says that money is no object and as far at the ATF is concerned, you let me worry about that."

Toulair's cell phone rang. He answered it and listened for a couple minutes without saying a word. He closed the call, returned the phone to his pocket, looked hard at Sorrell, and without a word he picked up his rifle, walked to his Humvee and drove off.

CHAPTER SEVEN

Monday, April 13

MAURY SPOONER CRUISED north on US Highway 63 in his two-year-old Mercedes. The Mercedes was Maury's one luxury even though he was two months behind on his lease payments. He loved his car. The Mercedes was on cruise control and Maury was on autopilot. He'd made the one hundred, three-mile trip from his office in Springfield to the South-Central Correctional Center just outside Licking, Missouri so many times it took no thought. His thoughts were focused on what he would say to his client. He knew from past experience that failure would not set well.

Since SCCC's visiting days were only on Thursdays through Sundays there was no line at the reception building. He once again endured the search, the metal detecting wand waved over his body and having his hand stamped, he finally arrived at the room set aside for inmates to meet with their attorneys.

Maury's client was ushered into the room by a

corrections officer. Neither the lawyer nor the inmate said a word until the CO left the room.

"Hello, Bella," Spooner said. "You're looking well," he lied. *She looks more haggard every time I see her.* She had lost weight, her skin had taken on the typical prison sallowness, and her hair was dingy and stringy.

She grunted and said, "Don't be a jerk. I look in the mirror and I know what I look like. But who's to care? Not me, that's for sure, not anymore."

"I'm afraid I have some bad news," Spooner said.

"Just what I need—my whole life is bad news."

"I'm sorry…"

"Skip it; I don't want your pity. Spit it out."

"My guy missed Grant. In fact, he died in the attempt."

The cold stare she gave Spooner sent chills up and down his spine. In a voice just as cold she said, "I don't care about the details; just tell me you got my money back."

"That would've been impossible. The cops got it."

"Was Grant even hurt?" she asked hopefully.

"Not a scratch. My guy just got off one round and that missed."

"Did Grant kill him?"

"Not exactly," Spooner said. "He shot out the back tire of the motor cycle my shooter was riding and he broke his neck in the crash. Pronounced dead on the spot."

"Well, at least we don't have to worry about him talking to the cops."

"He was a pro, but even pros mess up sometimes. What do you want to do now? You gonna give it up? That was a pretty expensive miss."

She stared at the little attorney for a long minute. "Not on your life. He put me in here and he is going to pay dearly for it." *I've got almost a million dollars stashed away and since it does me no good at all in here, if I have to I'll spend every dime of it to see Grant in his grave.*

"Do you have any more of your so called *pros*?" she asked. If her sarcasm registered on Spooner he didn't show it.

"Yeah, I think I can come up with one or two more. Same deal as before? Ten for him and ten for me?"

The money didn't matter to Bella Dubois-Barnes but the fact that Gideon Grant was alive and walking around free while she rotted in prison ate at her very soul. She was so consumed with hatred that it occupied nearly every thought of her mind. It kept her awake at night. She lay on her bunk in the dark cell dreaming and scheming of ways to make Gideon Grant suffer and die.

"That's what I'll do," she said almost to herself. "I'll make him suffer."

"What?" Spooner wasn't sure what she'd said.

"Get somebody good. But this time Grant's not the target. I want you to target someone he cares about. We'll make him suffer before he dies." Bella leaned across the table and whispered in Maury's ear and then sat back with a wicked smile on her face.

~~~~~

What little moral fiber Maury Spooner may have possessed as a young man disappeared a long time ago. *The idea of putting out contracts on people is sure not what I had in mind when I went to law school. But ten g's is ten g's.*

Driving west on Highway 60 almost to the Springfield city limits he picked up his cell phone from the passenger seat, scrolled down to the number he wanted and punched the green dial button. It was answered on the fourth ring. "Yeah?"

"It's Spooner, we need to talk."

A long string of expletives filled Spooner's ear. "Why should I want to talk to you? The last time we talked I
~~~~~

wound up doing five years in Licking."

"Look, I told you going in that with the evidence the PA had all I could do was try and get you a lighter sentence. Without me you'd of done ten to fifteen."

"Okay, okay. So what do you want to talk about?"

"Not over the phone. Meet me by the lake at Dowling Park at 10:00 tomorrow morning. I've got a proposition I think will interest you."

CHAPTER EIGHT

Monday, April 13

GRANT WONDERED ABOUT the mysterious call from Senator Gardner Burkes as he drove down the overcrowded Campbell Avenue toward the senator's large home in Nixa. He found the house with no difficulty using his GPS. The house was made of buff brick and stone with several gables. The yard had been recently mowed and featured several colorful flower beds and well-trimmed shrubs. *I'm glad I arrived a little early. It's always good to keep down surprises,*" Grant said to himself as he pulled onto the long driveway.

"Hmm, looks like Burkes had the same idea," he mused as he spotted a black Suburban parked in front of one of the three garage doors.

Grant parked behind the SUV, got out of his pickup and locked the door. He walked upon the porch and knocked on the solid oak door. He was greeted by a man wearing a black ski mask and holding a sawed-off double barrel shotgun. Before Grant could react the gun was shoved into his stomach.

"Get your hands up and get in here quick," said the masked man. "And keep your mouth shut or I'll blow you in two."

Knowing the damage a shotgun could inflict Grant obeyed. As he stepped into the house he quickly looked around. To his right was a room furnished as a living room. In the middle of the room he spotted Senator Gardner Burkes sitting in a straight backed chair. The Senator was bound hand and foot with duct tape which also covered his mouth. His eyes showed fear and panic.

As Grant started to ask what this was all about he received a blow to the back of his head and everything went black before he hit the floor.

~~~~~

Oh, man, my head is gonna explode, was his first thought as he regained consciousness. *Don't move—the guy with the shotgun may still be here.* He opened his right eye just enough to see if anyone was watching him. What he saw was his gun lying under his hand. Then he saw someone lying on the floor about six feet from him.

Senator Gardner Burkes lay in a pool of his own blood which drained from a hole in his head.

"Oh, for cryin' out loud—someone's trying to frame me for murder!"

The words were barely out of Grant's mouth when the door burst open and two uniformed police officers rushed into the room with revolvers in their hands. Grant turned on his side to look up at them. "I'm glad to see you guys," he said.

"Don't you move a muscle, Mister," the older of the two officers said. "Reed," he said to the other officer, "Keep him covered while I check out that guy over there—although it sure looks like he's dead."
~~~~~

"Okay, Everett," Reed said with a bit of quiver in his voice. "Good night, Mother, look at all that blood."

"Quit lookin' at the blood and watch this guy. If he twitches shoot him."

"Everett, don't you think it'd be a good idea to cuff him? He's as big as the two of us put together."

Everett turned from Burkes' body and said, "This guy sure ain't goin' nowhere. Mister, you get your hands behind your back."

Grant complied with the command and felt the handcuffs being clamped tightly on his wrists. "Can I sit up now? My head is killing me. Someone landed a good one on me when I walked in the door."

"Okay, but don't stand up. Just sit against the wall there so we can watch you better," Officer Everett Bond said. "Roy, get on your cell and call Lieutenant Cardswell. We're gonna have to have a lot of help with this mess. Do you know who the stiff is? He looks a little familiar but I can't place him."

"He's state Senator Gardner Burkes," Grant said.

"*The* Senator Burkes?" Everett and Roy said simultaneously.

"There's only one as far as I know," Grant said.

"Mister," Officer Roy Reed said, "you've got yourself in a real mess; killin' someone as powerful important as Senator Burkes. Yes, Sir, you're in real trouble."

"I didn't kill him, Officer. I just told you that someone knocked me out as I came through the door. He was alive then and tied to that chair over there. Someone shot him…probably with my gun…while I was out."

"A likely story," Everett said.

"Just take a close look at the evidence and you'll see I'm telling the truth."

"What evidence would that be?" asked another voice.

Bond and Reed jumped to attention as a man in civilian clothes walked into the room. "Lieutenant, am I glad to see you," Bond said. "We've got a real situation on our hands here." Pointing to the body on the floor, "This is, or was, that Senator Burkes you hear so much about on TV and in the papers."

The Lieutenant turned to Grant and asked, "Well, Mister, what do you have to say for yourself? Why'd you shoot the senator?"

"As I told the officers a while ago, I did not shoot Gardner Burkes. I had an appointment to meet him here at two o'clock today. I arrived a little early and when I knocked on the door some guy in a sky mask invited me in. And since he was holding a sawed-off double barreled shotgun against my stomach, I did just what he told me to. I walked in, saw Burkes tied to that chair and that's the last thing I remember 'til I woke up a while ago and saw Burkes lying in that pool of blood."

"My next question to you is this—who are you, Mister?"

"My name is Gideon Grant. I'm a private investigator from Springfield. Gardner Burkes and I played football together at MSU. We were never what you'd call *friends,* but he called me last Thursday and asked me to meet him here to discuss something he wanted me to investigate."

"What did he want you to *investigate*?" the lieutenant asked. The question dripped with sarcasm.

"He wouldn't discuss it over the phone and obviously he couldn't tell me about it today. I don't have a clue about what he wanted to discuss."

"All right," the lieutenant said, "let's see some ID."

"I figured you'd be asking for some. But when I reached for my wallet I discovered that it is missing," Grant said.

"How convenient."

"There's a spare set of ID in the glove box in my truck."

The lieutenant turned to Officer Reed, "Reed, go check it out."

"Yes, Sir, Lieutenant Cardswell," Reed said as he ran from the house to Grant's pickup. He was back in less than two minutes. “It ain’t there, Lieutenant. The window on the passenger side is busted out. Somebody must have taken his ID.”

Lieutenant Elgin Cardswell frowned and looked at Grant. “Well, Grant, or whatever your name is, I’m taking you in on suspicion of murder ‘til we can get this all sorted out. Hopefully you can corroborate the story you just told.

“Reed, take him out of here and put him in the back of my car and watch him ‘til I come out there.”

Realizing it was useless to argue Grant slowly got to his feet and walked to the unmarked Crown Vic.

Before he arrived at the car, thunder and lightning split the sky and rain began to pour on him and the police officer. *And I though it couldn’t get any worse,* he thought.

CHAPTER NINE

Tuesday, April 14, 9:35 a.m.

DOWLING PARK'S SMALL lake was more than a hundred years old. Years ago the park held an amusement park with rides, a tunnel of love and skating rink. All that was gone, replaced by a county run family recreation and aquatic center.

Maury Spooner arrived at the lakeside parking lot early since he had no other business to look after. *Gotta get me some more paying clients.* As he waited and watched for Byron Ledbetter he sipped coffee from a Styrofoam cup and ate his breakfast which he'd bought at McDonalds.

Maury dreaded facing Ledbetter for good reason. Even though he had been successful in obtaining a reduced sentence for the felon he knew the habitual criminal blamed him for having to spend four years in prison. He also knew that Ledbetter lived up to his reputation of being brutal in his punishment to those who were foolish enough to cross him. But he also knew that the six foot five, two hundred fifty-pound killer would do almost anything to earn

$10,000.

A dusty black five-year-old Town Car pulled in beside his Mercedes. The hulking Ledbetter exited his car, opened the passenger door of the Mercedes and grunted as he sat heavily next to Maury. He purposefully opened the lapel of his jacket to reveal the automatic pistol resting in a shoulder holster. He looked at Maury with a frown and said, "I don't have a lot of time to waste, Spooner. What you got that'll be worth my while?"

"I got a target that'll pay ten grand. Five now and five after it's done." *If he gets caught or killed I won't be out the whole ten g's.*

"Who's the target?"

Maury handed him a piece of paper. "Here's the name and address. Should be a piece of cake."

Ledbetter quickly looked at the paper and asked, "Does it matter how or when the hit is to happen?"

"All my client cares about is that it happens soon. The how is up to you. Just make sure it's permanent."

"I always do. Where's the five g's?"

"Open the glove box, it's in there."

Ledbetter popped open the door of the glove box and starred at the usual clutter found in them. "Okay, now what?"

Maury pointed at a white envelope and said, "It's in there. Count it if you like."

Ledbetter looked at the pudgy lawyer with a smirk, "Spooner, you may not be the brightest bulb on the lawyer chandelier but you've surely got enough smarts not to try and stiff me. Right?"

Maury tried to look and sound more confident that he felt. "It's all there and there's five more where that came from when the job's done."

Ledbetter slipped the envelop into his jacket pocket and reached for the handle of the car door. As he exited the car he said, "I'll be in touch."

When the hit man was out of sight Maury Spooner breathed a sigh of relief. *How did I let myself become so much like him? I hate what I'm doing, but I've got to have the dough. And the thought of winding up in Licking scares me half to death. I wouldn't last three days in there.*

CHAPTER TEN

Tuesday, April 14

BYRON LEDBETTER SPENT the better part of the morning shopping. His was a special kind of shopping as he sought an untraceable weapon with which to commit murder. He went to a couple pawn shops with no success. The owners were known to deal with such merchandise but currently had nonavailable. He finally found what he was looking for at Jason's Bar and Grill located just off the Square on College Street.

A booth in the rear of Jason's was the *office* of Fred 'Books' Miller. Fred was a bookie and loan shark who kept all his records in his head. He never put anything on paper, but he never forgot any of the details of his many transactions. Books wore an obvious and tacky hair piece and was obese to the extreme. He had in his employ certain men who insured that his loans and gambling debts were paid in a timely manner. Byron Ledbetter worked in that capacity from time to time so they were well acquainted.

Byron picked up two beers from the bar and carried

them to Books' booth and slid in across from the fat man. "How's it goin', Books?"

"Was goin' okay 'til you walked in. What you want?"

Ledbetter feigned being hurt, "Can't an old friend buy an old buddy a beer?"

"Yeah, right. As I said, what you want? You never come in here less you want somethin'."

"Okay, okay." Ledbetter leaned across the table and whispered, "I need an untraceable piece. You know where I can find one?"

"Depends on how much you're willin' to pay."

"Depends on what you got."

"A .38 revolver; guaranteed untraceable, seven 'c's."

"I could buy a brand new one for less than that," groused Ledbetter.

"It's the *untraceable* part that costs. Take it or leave it, makes no difference to me. You don't take it someone else will."

"When and where?" asked Ledbetter.

"Right here in one hour."

"See you soon," Ledbetter said as he slid out of the booth to leave.

An hour and ten minutes later he walked out of Jason's with the *guaranteed untraceable* .38 in his coat pocket. "Time to go huntin'."

CHAPTER ELEVEN

Tuesday, April 14

GIDEON GRANT LAY awake on the steel shelf that was supposed to be a bed in the Nixa Police Department's lockup. Even though Nixa was a fast-growing suburb just to the south of Springfield, he was unknown to the officers he had met thus far. The thin mattress between the cold steel and his body didn't help much. His head still throbbed. *I wonder when I'll get to make my phone call. And who should I call? Bernie Drake, Dick, Olga?* Bernie Drake was a friend and an attorney he'd worked with on a previous case. "What a mess!"

The Nixa cops had fingerprinted, searched him and booked him on suspicion of murder. They were courteous and professional about it.

It was a little after midnight when the steel door opened to reveal two jail guards. One held handcuffs in his hand and the other held a wooden club about two feet long. The guard with the cuffs said, "Stand up and turn your back to me so I can cuff you."

“Where we goin’?” Grant asked.

“You’ll know when we get there.”

“Okay, if you say so.”

“I say so, so just shut your trap.”

When the cuffs were in place the guard said, “You just follow me and don’t say nothin’ to nobody. Got it?”

“Got it,” Grant said.

The guard with the club walked a few paces behind Grant as they both followed the lead guard through several doors into the office area of the NPD. They stopped at a door with a name plate that read *Interrogation.* The lead guard opened the door and said, “Have a seat at the table in the chair that’s fastened to the floor.”

The interrogation room was sparsely furnished with a table in the middle of the room with three chairs. One chair, along with the table was indeed fastened to the floor, Grant saw, while the other two were loose on the opposite side of the table.

Grant sat where he was told and said, “Now what?”

“Now we wait.”

“For what?” Grant asked.

There was no reply from either guard as they took their place on either side of the door and leaned against the wall. They were clearly bored with the whole process.

Grant’s watch had been taken from him when he was booked so he guessed it was about twenty minutes later when the door opened and Detective Lieutenant Elgin Cardswell briskly walked in and sat in one of the chairs facing Grant.

“All right, Grant, your fingerprints confirm that you are who you say you are and that you have no record of any criminal behavior. So, do you want to talk to me or do you want to get a lawyer in here?”

Grant paused to frame his response. “Since I know that I did not kill Gardner Burkes and therefore have nothing to hide I’ll talk to you. If I decide I need a lawyer I’ll call one in Springfield."

"Okay," Cardswell said. He placed a small tape recorder on the table and turned it on. He stated his name, the date and time and purpose of the interrogation and the names of the two guards who were present. "So talk to me. What's your story about what happened yesterday afternoon at Senator Burke's house?"

"I've known the Senator, Gardner Burkes, since college days. We played football together at MSU. We were as well acquainted as anyone who played ball together for four years but never what you'd call friends. After college I joined the SPD and he joined the Army. I suspect you know his story; how he lost his legs and all that."

"Yeah, I know the story. He made sure everyone knew it."

"We never had any contact until he ran for the State Assembly from our district. He approached me about helping out in his campaign but I was committed to helping his opponent and told him so, and why."

Cardswell held up his hand for Grant to stop. "Why was that?"

"I didn't like his brand of politics. We were opposites on nearly every issue and I didn't like the way he manipulated people and his brand of the truth."

The detective motioned for him to continue his story.

"Last Thursday evening about eight o'clock he called me out of the blue—surprised me. He asked me to meet him at his house here in Nixa because he wanted me to look into something for him. Said he needed someone he could trust. Still wonder why he picked me. He was very mysterious about it. When I got his house I saw the SUV out front and figured he'd got there before me. When I knocked on the door it was opened by a man wearing a ski mask and holding a sawed-off shotgun in his hand. He ordered me in and since he had the shotgun jammed against my belly I followed him into the house. As soon as I stepped in I saw Gardner in the living room tied and gagged. Then somebody hit me in the back of the head and knocked me out. I woke up and saw my gun by my hand and Gardner lying in a pool of blood. My first thought was that I was being framed for murder. About that time your two officers arrived and you know the rest."

Cardswell had listened carefully to Grant's narrative. "And you have no idea as to why the Senator called you?"

"Not a clue."

"When did you last have any contact with the Senator?"

Grant thought for a moment. "Well, this is his third term in office and the last time I talked to him was before he was elected the first time. So, it's been about ten or twelve years."

"Does it seem strange that he'd call you after all this time?"

"Very strange; in fact it was downright weird."

Cardswell sat looking at Grant for a moment. "I'm tending to believe you, Grant, but I can't just let you walk out of here. It was your gun that killed Burkes and yours are the only prints on it. The knot on your head and the condition my officers found you in are in your favor."

"I appreciate your listening to my side of it," Grant said.

Cardswell handed Grant a cell phone and said, "Here, make your phone call. Hope whoever you call wont mind being woke up in the middle of the night."

"First," Grant said, "what do I need here? Corroboration or representation?"

"I think corroboration will do for now. "Who'll do that for you?"

"Do you know a Major Richard Jenkins of the SPD?"

"Not personally but I've heard a lot of good things about him."

"He and I were partners when I was a detective with SPD, and he's my best friend."

"Sounds like the man to call," Cardswell said.

Chapter Twelve

Tuesday, April 14, 10:00 a.m.

"I **REALLY APPRECIATE** your getting me out of that mess in Nixa," Grant said.

Major Dick Jenkins said, "I'm glad I could help. You gave me the short version last night; now give me the detailed version."

Grant filled Jenkins in on everything from Senator Burkes' phone call until Grant called Jenkins earlier that morning.

Jenkins said, "It sure would help if we knew why Burkes called you. It might help find the motive for his murder, and the attempt to implicate you."

"I know it's out of your jurisdiction but as you know, mine covers the whole state of Missouri. So I'll do some digging and then let you know what I find out. Until we find out who killed Burkes the folks in Nixa will continue to wonder about me."

~~~~~
~~~~~

During lunch at Ziggies, his favorite cafe, Grant struggled to keep from yawning as he repeated the story of his adventure in the neighboring city to June Whitlow.

"Are you sure you shouldn't have a doctor look at your head?" she asked.

"Naw, the Nixa PD had their doctor check it out before they released me. He thought it'd be all right."

"What are you planning to do next?" she asked.

"Try to find out what it was that Burkes wanted me to investigate for him."

~~~~~

Bert, the ever-efficient secretary, discovered that Senator Burkes' Springfield office was just a few blocks west of Grant and Oppermann Investigations on Battlefield Road. Gideon and Olga climbed into his truck and drove to the office which was located in a building that had formerly been a small dwelling. The building and grounds appeared to be well maintained.

Upon entering the front door they found two women sitting at desks talking on phones. The one nearest the door appeared to be in her fifties, tall and lean with a face that was so long it was unattractive, while the other was much younger, perhaps twenty-five and was short and about a hundred pounds overweight. The older woman finished her phone call, looked up at Grant and Olga with a slight smile and asked, "May I help you?"

Gideon handed the woman one of his cards and said, "My name is Gideon Grant and this is my partner, Olga Oppermann."

The woman gasped and said, "You're the one who was accused of killing Gardner!"

"Briefly accused," Grant said. "That's all been cleared up."
~~~~~

"Well, it's far from cleared up for us. We're going crazy with all these phone calls. People seem to think we know what's going on and we know next to nothing. No one is telling us anything."

Grant read the name on the plate on her desk: Norma Burkes. "How are you related to Gardner Burkes, Ma'am?"

"I'm his sister; his older and only sister." She pointed to the young woman at the other desk, "This is his niece, Ashton Burkes. My younger brother is her father."

"We are pleased to meet you both. And you have our deepest condolences in the loss of your brother and uncle."

"Thank you," Norma said. "It's been really hard on the whole family; especially the not knowing exactly what happened and why."

"I hope I can help a little. First of all, perhaps it might comfort you to know that he didn't suffer. That is he died instantly."

"What were you doing there, Mr. Grant?" Ashton asked. It was the first time she had spoken.

"Last Thursday evening Senator Burkes phoned me and asked that I meet him at his house in Nixa on Monday. He told me that he wanted me to look into something for him but he didn't want to discuss it over the phone. When I arrived I was greeted by a man in a ski mask and holding a shot-gun. Gardner was still alive when I got there. I was knocked unconscious and while I was out he was shot and killed...with my gun. The police took me in for questioning but later released me without charging me with any crime."

Norma's voice choked as she asked, "Did you ever find out what Gardner wanted you to investigate?"

"No. That's why we're here. We hoped you might shed some light on that."

"I don't have a clue," Norma said.

"Has anything unusual happened lately that might give you some kind of idea of what it was about?"

"Nothing I can think of," Norma said.

Ashton spoke up again, “What about that guy that came in talking real loud a couple weeks ago?”

“Girl, you talk too much,” Norma said. “You don’t tell office business to strangers.”

Ashton hung her head and said, “Yes, Ma’am, Aunt Norma.”

Grant sensed that they would gain nothing more by remaining any longer and turned to Olga, “Guess we may as well move on.”

Turning back to Norma he said, “Thank you for your help, and again you have our sympathy. We’ll remember you and your family in our prayers.”

Norma sniffed at that but Ashton said, “Thank you, we need all the prayer support we can get.”

~~~~~

Back in the truck Grant asked, “Well, what do you think about those two?”

“I think that Norma is holding something back, something that Ashton might be willing to tell us if she is asked properly.”

“That’s just what I think. The sign on the office door said that the office closes at 5:00. Why don’t you make a visit to Miss Ashton this evening?”

“I will look forward to it,” Olga said with a smile. “I will be near here at five and follow her home and we will have a little talk.”
~~~~~

CHAPTER THIRTEEN

Wednesday, April 15

OLGA DIDN'T HAVE to follow Ashton Burkes very far. She lived on the second floor of an apartment complex four blocks west of the late Senator's office. The building was constructed of brink and stone with cedar shake trimming. Olga gave her about five minutes, climbed the stairs and then knocked on her door.

Ashton was surprised to see the lady PI standing at her door. "Wha…what do you want?" She just stood there with her eyes open wide and her mouth hanging slack.

Olga smiled brightly and asked, "May I come in? I would like to ask you a few more questions." As she spoke she began moving forward forcing Ashton to step back.

Olga was a formidable force when she chose to be. The small apartment was neatly furnished with inexpensive furniture and was very clean.

Ashton closed the door and said, "I don't know what else I can tell you."

Olga looked down from her six feet height and starred

intently into the younger woman's eyes. "You know something about the matter your uncle called Mr. Grant about." It wasn't a question but a statement of fact.

Ashton averted Olga's piercing eyes and looked at the wall behind her. "I feel so disloyal. Aunt Norma wouldn't tell you guys the truth. I don't see why it should matter to her for you to know."

"Maybe we should sit down and talk about it," Olga said gently.

Ashton took two Cokes from her refrigerator and motioned for Olga to sit on the couch. She sat at the other end and struggled to pull her feet under her. "Uncle Gardner was a secretive man. He seemed to enjoy knowing stuff that nobody else knew; at least he thought nobody else knew." She paused to gather her thoughts and catch her breath.

"Go on," Olga said encouraging her.

"About two weeks ago a man came into the office when Uncle Gardner was there. He had called and spoken to Aunt Norma to make an appointment. I never did get his name but he was a little guy, about five feet, two and real skinny. Aunt Norma might give you the name since she made the appointment. But the little guy had a big booming voice. That's how I was able to hear what they talked about."

"Which was…?" Olga asked.

"I couldn't make it all out, but it had something to do with *guns.* That I'm sure of. I think the little man was asking Uncle Gardner to investigate something to do with guns."

Olga pressed her for more information. "Please, think carefully. Was there anything more that you heard that will tell us what the Senator was being asked to investigate?"

Ashton shook her head and said, "I'm sorry; I can't think of anything more."

Olga reached into her purse and took out one of her

business cards and handed it to Ashton. "Please call me if you think of anything else. It is very important. In fact, it might lead us to whoever killed your uncle."

"I really want his killer to be caught, so I'll think really hard about it. Okay?"

"Thank you very much," Olga said as she stood to leave.

~~~~~

As Olga entered the second-floor landing of the stairs she saw a very large man standing at the bottom of the next flight of stairs. The revolver seemed very small in his huge right hand. Before Olga could react he raised it and fired two rounds striking her in the chest and neck. Her purse was still open so as she fell backward onto the landing she instinctively reached for her .38 caliber Sig Sauer.

Blood was gushing from her neck wound and she knew she would soon be unconscious. She listened intently to the sound of footsteps on the stairs. *I must remain conscious. He must not get away.* With grim determination she raised her gun and waited for the shooter to appear on the stairs. As his head and shoulders rose into her sight it took all the strength she could muster to squeeze the trigger. Just as the .38 fired her strength gave out. Her arm dropped and Ledbetter took the round in his right shoulder rather in the head as she had intended. He yelped in pain and tumbled backward down the stairs. Grimacing in pain he staggered to his feet and stumbled out to his car. In less than three minutes after firing the first shot he was driving west on Battlefield and away from the scene of the crime. *I can't believe she shot me. Even after I put two rounds in her.*

Where can I go to get some help? Got to stop the bleeding.

~~~~~

Olga grabbed a handkerchief from her purse and pressed against her neck in an attempt to slow the flow of blood.

With her other hand she reached for her cell phone and pressed the speed dial button for Gideon Grant's cell phone.

He answered his phone on the first ring and noted Olga's name on the caller ID. "Yes, Olga."

"Gideon, help…me. I've been…shot…"

~~~~~

Grant stood and started walking toward the door and his truck. "Where are you?"

The only sound he heard was a weak groan. He turned back to Bert. "Bert, do you know where Olga was going when she left here?"

"Sure, to talk to Senator Burke's niece, Ashton—she lives just up the street in those new apartments."

"Olga's been shot. She must be there. Call 911 and get some help on the way," he shouted as he went out the back door.

As he ran to his pick-up he shouted into the cell phone, "Olga, can you hear me? Talk to me! Hang on, Olga, I'm coming."

Olga's voice came to his ear, stronger, "Oh, Gideon, I see…angels…"

"What? Angels?" He laid his head on the steering wheel and wept. *Oh, Lord, you've sent your angels for her. Thank you for letting me hear those words. Thank you for your wonderful salvation and the hope of heaven.*

He sped around his building and raced west on Battlefield and skidded to a stop on the curb in front of the apartments.

~~~~~

Ashton, too terrified by the gunfire to open her door, dialed 911 and reported what sounded like gun shots on the stairs of her apartment building. Unknown to her, several other tenants copied her action.

CHAPTER FOURTEEN

Wednesday, April 15

THE SPD DISPATCHER forwarded the 911 call to Officer Carl Walls who was cruising east on Battlefield about six blocks west of Ashton's apartment. Since gunfire had been reported he called for backup as he raced to the scene with lights flashing and siren screaming. He parked next to a black Ford pickup with one wheel up on the sidewalk.

The patrolman was cautiously approaching the stair well of the apartment building as two other black and white SPD units arrived. He paused to wait for the backup and then, with his weapon held out in front of him, he looked into the stairwell.

"Got some blood down here. Looks like somebody got hit hard."

"Up here! Get some help up here," Grant shouted. "My partner's been hit hard."

Officer Walls, still holding his weapon in front of him, walked up the stairs slowly. As his eye level cleared the second landing he called down the stairs to the other officers, "Someone's down up here—a woman."

"Move over, Mister, let me check her out."

He scrambled over to Olga's still body being careful not to step in the blood and placed his fingers on the side of her neck away from her wound. "She's gone."

Grant sat on the floor, leaned against the wall and cried, "Oh, nooo. Oh, Olga, Olga. I'm so sorry, I'm so sorry…."

Officer Walls looked at Grant and said, "I know you; you're that PI, Grant. Right?"

Grant just nodded and reached out to grasp Olga's limp hand. "She's my partner—and my friend." Tears rolled down his cheeks and he began to sob.

One of the backup officers was on his cell phone talking to their supervisor. "The woman is that PI's partner—Gideon Grant. He was here when we arrived; said she called him before she… expired."

The backup officer said, "Sergeant, you'll need to get in touch with Major Jenkins ASAP. He and Grant used to be partners and are good friends."

"Good idea," the sergeant said. "You guys secure the scene and don't let anybody even get close to it. CSI and some detectives are already on their way to you."

"Roger that. We'll take care of it."

Walls, the senior of the three responding officers said, "You guys get out the tape and start marking out the crime scene. I'll stay here with the victim. There's going to be a lot of questions asked about this and a lot of neighborhood canvassing to do."

He turned to Grant and said, "Mr. Grant, I'm very sorry for your loss. You're a former SPD detective aren't you?"

Grant spoke quietly, "Yeah."

"Well, then, Sir, you know that I've got to ask you to vacate the crime scene. We'll take good care of Miss Oppermann—I promise you that. The CSI unit will be here shortly." He reached for Grant's hand and pulled him to his feet.

With tears streaming down his face Grant stood looking down at Olga's body and the huge pool of blood. His voice choked as he said, "As God is my witness somebody's gonna pay, and pay dearly for this."

~~~~~
~~~~~

Gideon walked slowly to his pickup and got in. He sat behind the wheel and stared at nothing for several minutes. In a choked voice he said, “This is just too much…more than I can handle.” He pounded in the steering wheel and cried, “Oh, God, this hurts more than I can bear!”

He turned the key in the ignition and began driving west on Battlefield. He turned north on Campbell and drove into the lot of a liquor store he frequented in his days as a drunk.

He walked out of the store with a brown paper bag which held a large bottle of Jack Daniel’s whiskey. *This used to take away the pain.*

He drove west out of town to a wooded area and parked on the side of the road. He got out of the truck and walked blindly into the woods to a rocky outcrop and several fallen trees. He sat on one of the logs and pulled the bottle from the bag. His hands were shaking so badly he couldn’t get the cap off the bottle.

He held the bottle up toward the sky and let the sun shine through the amber liquid fire. An inner voice said, *“What are you doing?”*

“I’m running away from the pain…from the guilt.”

“Did booze ever really take away the pain?”

“It helped to forget for a while.”

“What guilt are you running from?”

“I shouldn’t have sent her to talk to Ashton alone. We’re partners.”

“She would have resented you not trusting her to do her job.”

Gideon cried aloud, “But she’s gone…dead…and I feel so helpless, so alone…”

“Remember that verse in the Psalms: “God is our refuge and strength, a very present help in trouble.”?”

Gideon crawled off the log and knelt on the grass and fallen leaves. “Oh, my father, forgive me for what I was about to do. I promised you and a lot of people that I would never touch anther bottle of booze. Oh, God, please help me. I am so weak…I’m so…angry.”

Another passage of Scripture came to his mind, *“Without me you can do nothing.”*

“I know that, Lord.”

“I can do all things through him who strengthens me.”

He looked at the bottle in his right hand like he was holding a rattlesnake. He suddenly drew back his arm and threw the bottle as hard and as far as he could against the rocks a few yards away. He rose shakily to feet and looked up into the clear blue sky. Tears rolled down his face as he said, "Thank you, Lord, for your blessed Holy Spirit who reminded me of these scripture verses. Thank you for your presence and help. And now, O God, help me find Olga's killer."

~~~~~

A grief-stricken Major Richard Jenkins drove quickly to the offices of Grant and Oppermann Investigations. When Bert saw his grim face she knew at once that something was gravely wrong.

"It's Olga, isn't it?" she asked.

"Yes, Bert," Jenkins said huskily, "is Gideon in?"

"No, Sir, Major; Olga called him and he rushed out of here saying something about her being shot. Are you telling me that she didn't make it?"

"I'm afraid so. She lost too much blood too fast. Nothing could be done in time."

They heard the back door open and looked to see Gideon walk in the office door. His face was as white as a sheet and his hands, shirt and trousers were covered with Olga's red blood. He stood looking at Jenkins for a long moment before anyone spoke. "Why, Dick?" he asked with a sob. "Why Olga? What am I gonna do without her? She's…was…my partner."

Jenkins spoke gently, "There's no real answer to 'why.' You know that. It's the same as when Malcomb Lancaster and Bonnie Wilks were killed. It's the tragic reality of *evil* in the world we live in"

Grant looked at Jenkins a long time before he answered. "Yeah, you're right, as always. We may never know why but you better believe that I *will* find out *who* is responsible."

They moved to Grant's office where he sat behind his desk. Jenkins sat in one of the guest chairs and Bert went to get three cups of coffee.

Tears filled Jenkins eyes as he said, "It looks like someone
~~~~~

ambushed her—shot her twice; once in the chest and one in the neck. Before she died she got off one round. From all the blood at the bottom of the stairs she must have made a solid hit."

Grant opened his mouth to say something but all that came out was an anguished cry. "Ohhh, God in heaven, whyyy? Why Olga? Why not me?" He put his face in his hands and leaned on his desk and sobbed. Bert moved to his side and put her arms around him and wept with him.

After a couple moments Grant raised his head and said, "I should have stayed at the scene, Dick. She was my partner, my friend. I owe it to her to find the person or persons responsible for this."

"I know how you must feel, Gideon," Jenkins said. "But Phil and the rest of my guys are doing everything necessary. You know the importance of preserving a murder scene and gathering all the evidence. There's nothing you could do there that CSI won't do."

Grief stricken, Grant laid his head on his desk again. After a few minutes Grant suddenly sat up with a strange kind of smile on his face. "She's in heaven! Dick, she's in heaven. She trusted Jesus last August right here. June and Bert took her and Betsy to see *The Passion of the Christ* and they both prayed to receive Christ. I heard them pray and we all danced around and hugged and cried. Do you know the last thing she said to me on the phone?"

"Well, no—what was it?"

"Angels, she said she saw angels. It's just like the Bible says. Jesus sent his angels to take her to heaven." Grant's voice choked again. "Is that great or what?"

"Great doesn't even begin to cover it. Knowing Jesus makes all the difference in life, and in death," Jenkins said.

Choked with emotion Grant said, "I don't know how I'm going to get along without her, but knowing she's with the Lord sure makes this easier to bear."

They heard the front door of the office open and looked up to see June Whitlow and Ellen Jenkins rushing in together. They both rushed to Gideon and put their arms around him. June said, "Oh, Gideon, I'm so sorry. I know how much she meant to you."

Grant just clung to June and Ellen and wept—his tears falling into their hair.

Bert, the great prayer warrior, said, "I think it's time for us to practice A.S.A.P. Always Say A Prayer." The five of them joined hands in a small circle beside Grant's desk and bowed their heads. Bert began to weep and pray, "Oh, Lord God of heaven and earth, we come to you with our pain and sorrow at the loss of our dear sister, Olga. Lord, as you know, we're very angry about this…we don't understand it…we don't like it…we're having a hard time accepting it. Your Word tells us that "all things work together for good to those who love you, to those who are the called according to your purpose." We sure can't see what good can ever come from this but we are trusting you to make it happen in your own way and in your own time. Please help us, Lord. We can't bear this pain and this grief in our own strength."

She paused and continued, "Now, we thank you and praise you for the assurance that Olga is with you, in your very presence simply because she put her trust in you to forgive her sins and save her for time and eternity. Thank you for Olga's dying testimony about your holy angels coming for her. Thank you for the promise of your comfort in times like this, we're countin' on you, Lord, because we've got nowhere else to turn. In Jesus name we pray, Amen."

All the rest of the group said, "Amen."

~~~~~

After Dick Jenkins had left to go back to the crime scene and June went back to the Justice Center, Grant and Bert sat for several minutes without saying a word. Grant broke the silence, "We've got to let Betsy and Joe Bob know. Betsy is going to be absolutely crushed by this."

Betsy Oppermann, an MP in the U. S. Army stationed at nearby Fort Leonard Wood, was Olga's cousin and dearest friend. They had been reunited the past summer after losing track of each other when they emigrated to the U.S. from Germany. Joe Bob, Joseph Robert Rounds, a Greene County Sheriff's Deputy, was Olga's nephew.

"I'll call Betsy's CO, Major Barkley, and have him take a
~~~~~

chaplain with him to tell her. I'd like to go myself but my first and most important task is to track down the… I don't know what to call him, or them! I want to curse and swear and scream. But I know that won't help."

The office door opened again; this time it was the Transitional Pastor, Jack Wallace, and several members of Highland Baptist Church, where Grant was a member. Deacon Dick Jenkins had called them. Olga and Betsy Oppermann had been baptized at HBC the previous year and were also members of that fellowship. Grant breathed a silent prayer, "Thank you, Lord, for the help and comfort of having a church family."

CHAPTER FIFTEEN

Wednesday, April 15

DRIVING TOWARD HIS office on Commercial Street, Maury Spooner grinned in anticipation of billing some hours to two clients he'd signed up; one at the Doctor's Hospital and the other at the Southside Police Station. The country music playing on the radio of his Mercedes was interrupted with the local news on the hour. "A female private investigator, Olga Oppermann, was found shot to death in the stairwell of an apartment building on East Battlefield. Police spokesperson, Shelly Krim, stated that it appears that the person who shot Oppermann was also shot. According to our sources, Private Investigator Oppermann was shot twice, but before she died she shot whoever ambushed her. She lived long enough to call her partner, Gideon Grant. Police are continuing their investigation into the shooting."

Spooner slapped the steering wheel and swore. He said, "I've got to find Ledbetter quick. If the cops get to him first he'll take me down with him. But at least my client's wishes were carried out. Guess I better go see her again. Wonder what she'll want to do now."

~~~~~

Spooner's client, Inmate Number 251350 of the SCCC, Licking, Missouri, aka Bella Dubois-Barnes, was ecstatic about his report. "Now we're getting somewhere. If Grant thinks he's suffering now he's got another think coming."

Maury Spooner was very uncomfortable contemplating what Bella had next in mind. *This is getting way out of hand. Tax free money is one thing but this could wind up with me locked up in here with this nut.*

Bella sat across the table from Spooner and rubbed her hands together with a wide grin on her face. "I want you to arrange to take out at least one more person before we get to Grant himself."

"I don't know," Mr. Ireland. "This is getting too risky for my blood."

"I'll make it worth your while. I'll double the money. Will that make it worth the risk?"

Spooner didn't recognize what was happening to him, but *greed* was distorting his thinking and taking control of his life. He was about to learn that indeed the love of money is the root of all kinds of evil.

"Tell you what," Bella said, "I'll make it fifty thousand for you. You spend whatever you have to to make it happen and keep the rest for yourself. Deal?"

All Spooner could think of was what fifty thousand dollars would do for his cash flow problems. "Deal, who do you have in mind?"

Bella thought for a moment. "Let me make it easy for you. There are at least four people we can choose from; his girlfriend who prosecuted me and put me in this hell hole, his secretary, or either of his parents. Any one of those will do the job of making Grant suffer. Then it's his turn."
~~~~~

Spooner thought, *I might as well strike while the iron is hot.* "It'll cost you a hundred Gs for Grant."

Bella didn't even blink. "Not a problem."

~~~~~

Looking into the sun as he drove west toward Springfield Spooner pondered his problem. *Ledbetter, wherever he is, probably out of commission for a while. Who else do I know that can and will do the job...cheap?*
~~~~~

CHAPTER SIXTEEN

Wednesday, April 15

OLGA OPPERMANN'S NEPHEW, Sheriff's Deputy Joe Bob Rounds, picked up the news of her death from the chatter on the radio of his Greene County Sheriff's patrol car. He immediately called his supervisor and requested permission to leave his patrol area and go check on the situation surrounding his aunt's death.

The SPD Crime Scene Investigation officers sympathized with Joe Bob but would not allow him to enter the crime scene. Dejected he made his way east on Battlefield to the offices of Grant and Oppermann Investigations. He had seen Grant a few times since the funeral service of his mother, Ingrid Oppermann Rounds, in June of the previous year.

Bert recognized Joe Bob as he walked through the office door. "Oh, Joe Bob, I'm so sorry about dear Olga."

"Thank you, Mrs. Young. Do you know what happened? SPD was short on details."

Gideon had heard the exchange and walked from his office. He gave Joe Bob a huge hug and said, "Come on into my office and I'll tell you what little I know. Bert, would you get us some fresh coffee, please Ma'am?"

"Of course. Joe Bob, a lot of people are already praying for you and Betsy."

"I appreciate that," he said. He turned to Gideon, "Has Betsy been notified?"

"Yes," Grant said. "I just got off the phone with her. Her CO and a chaplain are with her. She'll come down tomorrow. It'll be up to you and Betsy to make the funeral arrangements."

"Oh, man, I don't have a clue what to do. Olga took care of everything for Mom."

"I'll go with you, and it might be a good idea to ask Brother Jack Wallace, our Transitional Pastor to help. He'll know what to do. I hate to say it, but in a case like this there'll have to be an autopsy. So it'll be a few days before funeral arrangements can be made. If you'd like, I'll keep track of that and let you and Betsy know when we can go the funeral home."

Joe Bob breathed a deep sigh and said, "Thanks, that'd help a lot."

"You want to use Decker Funeral Home? They did your Mom's service."

"Sure, they were really helpful."

Gideon sat in his desk chair and waved Joe Bob to one of the chairs in front of his desk. Bert placed cups of coffee in front of each man.

They sat in silence for a moment, and then Joe Bob asked, "Now, what happened? *How* could this happen?"

"Evidently she was ambushed by somebody. She'd just left the second-floor apartment where she'd been questioning a lady about a case we're working on. She took two rounds—one in the chest and one in the neck."

Grant choked up and had to stop for a moment. "It was

probably the neck wound that was fatal. Exsanguination was rapid. Before she died she shot whoever shot her. Then she was able to dial my number on her speed dial. Told me she's been shot and needed help. By the time I got there it was too late to help her."

"But why would someone be after Aunt Olga? That doesn't make any sense."

"My guess is that it was just a hired gun. And just *who* he is and who hired him is going to be the entire focus of my life until I find who it is and take him down," Grant said vehemently.

"I want in on it," Joe Bob said quietly. "She was family—apart from Betsy all the family I had. Except for Dad of course, but the State of Texas locked him up and threw away the key."

Joe Bob stood up to leave. "I've got to get back out on patrol; we're running short handed, as usual."

"After the funeral we'll get our heads together with Dick Jenkins and see what we can do. Okay? And once again, I am so sorry for your lose, and mine. I loved her like the sister I never had."

They hugged and slapped each other on the back and Joe Bob left.

~~~~~

Gideon picked up his phone and dialed the number of June Whitlow's direct line from memory. Her caller ID caused her to say, "Hello, Darling. Are you all right?"

"No, and I won't be for a long time. I'm afraid this may put our wedding plans on hold for a while."

"That's the least of our worries right now. But knowing Olga, I doubt she'd want to be the cause of delaying our wedding. We'll work it all out."

"Okay, if you say so. Can you get away for Prayer Meeting with me tonight? I need to be with some praying
~~~~~

people. I'm having a really hard time dealing with the desire for vengeance and I know the Bible says that's wrong."

"The whole church prayer chain has been praying for you and Betsy ever since it happened. Why don't you let me pick you up and take you to supper before church?"

"That would be nice--about five thirty at my place?"

"See you then. Oh, by the way, have you talked to your folks about Olga? They thought an awful lot of her."

"Not yet. I'll run over there right now."

In a soft voice June said, "I love you, Sweetheart. With the Lord's help we'll get through this together."

"Yeah, I know. I love you, too." *I wish I was as confident as you are, Love.*

~ ~ ~ ~ ~

By the time Gideon arrived at his parents' home they had already learned about Olga's death. They did all they could to comfort and reassure him. He didn't stay long as he needed to get home to walk and feed Bruno before he showered and changed to go supper and Prayer Meeting with June.

~ ~ ~ ~ ~

During the Prayer Meeting Pastor Wallace had Gideon to come to the front of the sanctuary and invited any of the people who desired to come and lay hands on him as they prayed for him and for Olga's remaining family. Soon Gideon was surrounded by his brothers and sisters in Christ. The pastor lead the prayer, "Father, we come to you in Jesus' name. Thank you for allowing us into your holy presence. Thank you that Jesus, your Son, is at your right hand interceding for us even now. Thank you that your Holy Spirit is in us to help us as we pray because we really need your help right now. Lord, we don't understand why things like this happen. We know and believe that you are the sovereign Lord of the universe. So, even in the face of evil we put our trust in you.

"Lord, in this moment of grief and sorrow, and in the midst of all our unanswered questions, we lift up Gideon and Betsy and Deputy Rounds to you asking that you do a work in their lives that only you can do. We ask that you give them comfort, strength and direction for the days ahead. Thank you for every promise of your Word. By faith we claim them. For every blessing you bring we give you honor, glory and blessing. In Jesus name we pray, Amen."

CHAPTER SEVENTEEN

Thursday, April 16

DETECTIVE LIEUTENANT ELGIN Cardswell of the Nixa PD stood in front of the desk of the Christian County Prosecuting Attorney, Mary Matthews. Mary had overcome many obstacles to reach her present position, especially the county's old boy network, and she was determined to do her job beyond the expectations of the people of Christian County.

"Tell me again," Lieutenant, "why you allowed this Gideon Grant to walk away from this *very* possible homicide indictment."

"Number one, the circumstances present at the scene lead me to believe Grant was being set up. Number two, I believed his story. Number three, Major Jenkins of the SPD said that there was no way Grant would assassinate anyone, much less a State Senator."

"In his *opinion*," Matthews said in a voice dripping with sarcasm. She opened a file lying on her desk. "According to *your* report he had means and opportunity, and his fingerprints were on the murder weapon—his weapon."

"Yes, Ma'am, that's what it says, but it's all too pat, too neat to be real. I still think he was set up by someone who lured Grant to that house and waited for him to arrive."

"Then can you answer three questions for me?"

"I'll certainly try," Cardswell said. *If you'd take my word for this I could get back to work trying to find the real killer.*

"Who, how and why? Who lured Grant to the senator's house, how did they do it and why, what was the motive?"

"I can only tell how? Grant received a call from Senator Burkes," Cardswell pulled a small notebook from his coat pocket and flipped a few pages, "on Thursday evening, April 9, at about 7:10 p.m. The Senator asked Grant to come to his house in Nixa on Monday to meet with him; and that he wanted Grant to look into something that happened in Springfield for him. He wouldn't say what it was over the phone. The rest is in the report."

"And you fell for this cock and bull story? A man with your *experience?* Really, Lieutenant, what were you thinking?"

"Based on my *experience* and my investigation, I believed his story—still do."

"What investigation?"

"The crime scene investigation to begin with. Grant was just regaining consciousness when the first officer arrived. He had a big lump on the back of his head. His wallet with his ID was missing and his truck had been broken into and his backup ID removed. Why would he do that to himself—makes no sense. CID checked Grant's hands for g.s.r. and found none. They checked Senator Burkes' wrists, face and those prosthetic legs of his and found residue of duct tape which corroborates Grant's account of his being bound in a chair when he first arrived. All that plus Grant's reputation and what Major Jenkins said."

Cardswell could tell from the look on Matthews face

that she wasn't buying it. "I've got to prosecute someone for this murder. It's too high profile to let it go unsolved, and in my book, Grant looks good for it."

"In my opinion you're barking up the wrong tree."

"All right, just for argument's sake, if Grant was, as you say, set up for it, who did kill Burkes and frame Grant?"

Cardswell said, "I've discovered that Grant has recently been instrumental in sending some very high profile, wealthy people to prison. There was an attempt on his life early on the morning that Senator Burkes called him. And to top it all off, just this morning Grant's partner was murdered."

Matthews sat up straight at that news. "Murdered? How?"

"Don't know all the details—just that she was shot just a few blocks from their office."

"She? His partner was a woman?"

"That's the word I got."

Mary Matthews sat thinking for a moment before continuing. "All right, we'll not indict Grant—for now. But I'm not making any promises about later. Get me a killer. The mayor is breathing down my neck, and he's got the Leader of the Senate and the governor's office breathing down his neck. Burkes was not only a powerful and influential senator, he was a war hero. Both his legs were blown off in Iraq."

"Yeah," Cardswell said, "the news media has him ready for sainthood, but the word around town and in Jeff City is that he was anything but a saint."

"I don't care what the media says and I haven't got time to waste on rumors. Get me some evidence that will lead to an indictment. And I really don't care who—just get me somebody!"

Matthews stood indicating that the meeting was terminated and Cardswell left her office.

~~~~~

APA Mary Matthews waited a few minutes after Cardswell exited her office and then pulled her cell phone from her purse. She dialed a number from memory and when a voice answered she said, “I’m sorry, but it’s not going to stick to Grant. Your guys were too sloppy.”

The reply she received made her blush, and she thought she had heard it all.
~~~~~

CHAPTER EIGHTEEN

Thursday, April 16

GIDEON SAT AT his desk staring at the wall thinking about the just completed phone call from Lieutenant Cardswell. If I'm ever going to get the suspicion that I killed Burkes off my back, the real killer's going to have to be found. But for now I'll have to leave that up to Cardswell. Olga's murder is my main concern for the time being.

He picked up his phone again and dialed Major Dick Jenkins direct line. When Dick answered he asked, "Have your guys come up with any new information on Olga's murder?"

"Most of the residents in the building that were home at the time heard the shots but were too afraid to venture out of their apartments to investigate. All they could do was help establish the time. The neighborhood canvass didn't turn up anything. So far no one saw anything unusual."

"That's about what I expected. Let me know if anything interesting turns up."

"Of course. Is there anything Ellen or I can do to help you?"

"Betsy's coming in today. If Ellen could visit with her I'm sure that would help. This is going to be especially hard on her. They were so very close."

"Let us know when and where."

"Thanks, Dick. Keep praying for me. I'm having a really hard time with my anger…and I might as well admit…my desire for *revenge*. It's eating me up."

"Of course. If you'll remember, we both had that problem when Pastor Lancaster was killed."

"Yeah, that was the first time someone so close to me was murdered. This is even worse, Olga was my *partner*."

"I fully understand. We'll get to the bottom of this, don't worry. I will keep you informed of our progress. What are you going to do next?"

"I'm going to start by talking to those two women at Burkes' office again."

~~~~~

The late Senator Gardner Burkes' sister and secretary, Norma, and his niece, Ashton, were both on the telephone when Grant entered the office. They appeared to be harried and near tears. Norma waved him to a chair near her desk.

She was saying, "I don't have access to that information. You'll have to contact the Nixa Police Department."

When she hung up the phone she turned to Grant with a sigh and said, "It's been a madhouse here ever since Gardner's death. Everybody wants information—something we still have very little of, I'm sorry to say."

She reached out her hand and laid it on his arm. "I'm so sorry about your friend. And Ashton is beside herself about it—Miss Oppermann had just left her apartment when she was shot."

"Yes, that's why I'm here. I need to know what Miss
~~~~~

Burkes told Olga."

"She'll be off the phone in a minute or two."

When Ashton hung up her phone she stood and walked to where Grant was sitting. Tears welled up in her eyes as she said, "I'm so sorry about Miss Oppermann. She was very nice to me. It was horrible—what happened to her I mean. I heard the shots but I was too terrified to go outside my apartment."

"You were right not to go out. You had no idea who was out there or if the shooting was over. You could have been injured or killed yourself. So don't feel bad about staying in your apartment," Grant said in a gentle voice.

"I saw all the blood afterward. It made me sick—I've never seen anything like it and I hope I never do again."

"Miss Burkes, I need…"

She interrupted him, "Please call me Ashton."

"All right. Ashton, I need you to tell me about your conversation with Olga in your apartment."

"I'll try to remember. She said that I knew something about Uncle Gardner's business that I didn't tell you when you were in the office with her yesterday. I told her that Uncle Gardner was a secretive man…"

Barbra interrupted her, "You're still talking too much, girl."

"Please, Miss Burkes," Gideon said, "it's important that I hear what Ashton told Olga.

Ashton continued, "Anyway, he liked to keep secrets. There was this man who came to talk to him. He was a little guy, about five feet two and real skinny. But he had a loud, booming voice. That's how we could hear what they were talking about back in Uncle Gardner's office. It was something about *guns*. It sounded like the man wanted Uncle Gardner to investigate something about guns." She turned to Norma, "Isn't that what we heard, Aunt Norma?"

Norma sniffed and made it clear that she didn't want to participate in the conversation. But she said, "Yes, that's what it sounded like—something to do with guns."

Grant sat quietly for a moment before he spoke. "Guns? And it was a little guy with a big voice that talked to Gardner? But you didn't get his name?"

"Well, I have it now," Norma said. "I got it off Gardner's calendar."

"I need that name," Grant said.

"It's Roger Addison. He owns and operates a gun repair shop in Republic. That's all I know about him."

"That's exactly what I need to know, thank you," Grant said as he stood to leave.

CHAPTER NINETEEN

Thursday, April 16

CHRISTIAN COUNTY PROSECUTOR Mary Matthews sat with her elbows on her desk and her head in her hands. How'd I get myself in such a mess? Money, you idiot, it's always money. This was supposed to be easy money. It sounded so good, so foolproof. Stupid, stupid, stupid!

Matthews divorced her cheating husband two and a half years ago and since she made a lot more money than her ex did the judge who sat on the case awarded *him* alimony. That plus the fact that she was still paying off her divorce attorney caused her to always be short of money.

Her conscience was untouched about setting Senator Gardner Burkes up to be murdered. *That slime ball led me on for almost a year and then dumped me for that bimbo secretary of his. Well, Senator, you messed with the wrong woman. You got just what you deserved.*

"But," she said quietly to herself, "I've put myself between the proverbial rock and a hard place. Morgan

Toulair on one side and the law on the other, and I'm much more concerned about Toulair than the law."

Toulair's proposal offered a solution to her money problems. He promised to pay her $25,000 cash for her part in setting up Burkes for the hit and Gideon Grant as the fall guy...just because Burkes had called Grant for some reason. *I doubt that I'll ever see a penny of that.* She began to pace around the office talking softly to herself. "It would have worked if Toulair had enlisted some competent help. Those two bozos were useless, and even worse, now they're potential witnesses against Toulair. And that is a position I would not want to be in for any amount of money."

Matthews picked up her phone and dialed the number of Senator Gardner Burkes' office in the State Capitol building in Jefferson City. The late Senator's secretary, Alexandria, answered on the first ring, "Senator Burkes' office."

"Alex, Mary Matthews here. I'm terribly sorry about the death of Senator Burkes, especially to die like that."

"It's horrible. I've never known anyone who was murdered before."

"I'm calling about our conversation on Wednesday, the eighth of April. Do you recall it?"

"I think so. What about it?"

"I'll make it well worth your while to *forget it ever happened.* Do you understand what I mean?"

"Yeah, I guess so. Exactly what do you mean?" Alex asked.

"You're going to be looking for another job soon and you'll probably need some cash to carry you 'til you find something. I'll give you, say $2500, and put in a word for you at the Cole County PA's office. I happen to know they're looking for a good secretary."

"All that for *forgetting* a phone call?"

"Yes," said Mary Matthews. *And hopefully to keep me from going to prison, or worse, end up dead.*

"Okay, I guess I can do that," Alex said while wondering what could be so important about her telling the PA about the call Senator Burkes made to Gideon Grant, whoever he is.

CHAPTER TWENTY

Thursday, April 16

BERT LOOKED UP the address and phone number of Roger Addison's gun shop on her computer and gave Gideon a printout of the required information. It was another beautiful spring day in the Ozarks. *It's good to be outside. Oh, Olga, I miss you so much.* The drive to the shop took him about twenty minutes. He arrived at the shop at a little past two in the afternoon. It was a standalone building located in a residential area of modest homes. Addison was busy with a customer when he entered so he spent some time looking around at the various firearms on display. The gun shop was immaculately clean and the weapons on display were conveniently arranged with trigger guards in place.

As the customer exited the shop Addison stepped toward Grant and said, "May I help you, Sir?"

Grant smiled and said, "I hope so." He pulled one of his business cards from his shirt pocket and handed it to Addison. "I'm Gideon Grant, a private investigator from

Springfield."

Addison stepped back and stared up into Grant's face. "I thought I recognized you. You're the guy they thought killed Senator Burkes. I don't want any trouble, Mister."

"Relax, Mr. Addison. I'm certainly not here to cause you any trouble. I'm investigating the murder of the Senator and the murder of my partner, Olga Oppermann."

"Oh, yeah, I saw that on the news. Sorry about your loss."

"Mr. Addison," Grant said, "let me tell you a story." He began with Senator Gardner Burkes' telephone call asking him to come to Nixa and told him most of everything that happened until Ashton Burkes gave him Addison's name.

"Wow," Addison said in his booming voice, "that's quite a tale. But why have you come to see me?"

"Please don't try to be coy with me, Addison. I know that you went to see Senator Burkes and talked to him about wanting him to investigate something to do with guns. That's what started this whole mess. So let's have it. What was it you wanted Gardner to look into?"

Addison's lower lip began to tremble but then he quickly drew in a deep breath and said, "Look, Mr. Grant, I don't know you and for all I know you're a killer. So why don't you just leave me alone?"

Not to be sidetracked so easily, Grant said, "I tell you what. Why don't we start all over again? Okay?"

Addison just looked at him not saying a word.

This is not going well, Grant thought. *What can I say to gain his confidence?* Then it came to him. "Do you know Assistant Police Chief Jimmy Young here in Republic?"

"Yeah, I've met him on occasion. Don't know him well though."

"Do you trust him to tell you the truth?" Grant asked.

"I guess so…yeah, I believe I do."

Grant sighed with relief. "Will you call him and ask his opinion of me and my reputation?"

"I'll have to look up his number," Addison said tentatively.

"Don't bother; I've got it in my cell phone." Grant pulled out his phone and punched the keys for his address book. He handed the phone to Addison who read the number aloud as he punched it into his phone and put it on speaker.

It took a couple minutes to get through to Jimmy Young. "Chief Young, you may not remember me but I'm Roger Addison. You were in my gun shop a few months ago for some repair work."

"Yes, I remember, Mr. Addison. What can I do for you?"

"I have a private investigator in my shop named Gideon Grant. He wants some sensitive information from me but I don't know how reliable he is. He suggested that I call you—that you'd vouch for him."

Grant could hear Jimmy Young laughing into the phone. Young then said, "Yes, I can vouch for Gideon. In fact, my wife is his secretary. She thinks he hung the moon. He's as straight a shooter as they come. I would trust him with my life. Shoot, I trust him with my *wife* every workday. If you're in trouble you couldn't have a better man on your side."

"Thank you, Chief," Addison said softly. "Thank you very much." He hung up.

Addison walked to the front door of his shop, locked it and turned the "OPEN" sign around so that the "CLOSED" sign was exposed to the outside. "Let's go back to my office so we can talk in comfort. Coffee? Coke?"

Gideon breathed a silent prayer of gratitude for friends like Jimmy Young as they walked through the door in the rear of the shop into a small but well-furnished office. He said, "Coffee would be great, thanks." Addison motioned Grant to a chair in front of his small desk as he moved to a coffee maker on the cabinet countertop behind the desk.

When he'd placed two mugs of coffee on the desk he took a seat behind the desk.

"Here's what I'm worried about, Mr. Grant. I don't know a whole lot, but what I do know scares me down to my toes. I go to a lot of gun shows and I hear a lot of stuff. Being around guns all my life as a Marine and a repairman my natural hearing is pretty poor. But, as you can see, I wear two hearing aids; and these buggers are super sensitive. I can hear stuff most people can't. Three weeks ago I was at a show at the Empire Fair Grounds in Springfield. I had a booth but after a few hours I got tired of sittin' so I wondered around a while."

Addison gulped down some coffee and continued. "I was readin' some info in the NRA booth when I overheard three men talking on the other side of the booth. They couldn't see me but I could hear them real good. They were negotiating a deal for five Barrett 50-caliber sniper rifles."

"I'm sorry," Grant said, "but I'm not familiar with the weapon. I do know that 50-caliber is a huge bullet."

"To say the least," Addison said. "I happen to have one in the work room in back of the shop if you'd like to see it."

"You bet."

They got up and Grant followed Addison to a workroom at the rear of his building. Addison stopped in front of a large rifle, spread his arms and said, "There she is—the Barrett 50-Caliber Sniper Rifle, or the M82A1A in Marine Corps parlance. That is a sniper's dream weapon. Twenty-eight and a half pounds unloaded; fifty-seven inches long; mounted on a bipod; has an accurate killing range of 2,000 yards and will send a projectile over 7,400 yards at 2,000 yards per second. Has a magazine that holds ten Mark 211, 660 grain, armor piercing, incendiary, explosive rounds. All that, combined with a carbide penetrating core will blow a hole through one inch armor plate or a three-and-a-half-inch manhole cover. So you see it's a weapon you don't want to fall into the wrong hands."

"Good night Gert, who can legally own such a weapon?" Grant asked.

"Anybody with a license. The military is the main user, of course, but some law enforcement agencies have them for special operations—Swat Teams, people like that. But most city and county cop shops can't afford 'em. They're super expensive."

"From what you've told me," Grant said, "I'm assuming Senator Burkes was going to ask me to look into the information you gave him."

"That'd be my guess. Where do you start on something like this?"

"First of all, do you have any idea who the people were that you overheard talking at the gun show?"

"Not for sure, but one of the voices sounded familiar. I wouldn't swear to it, but I'm pretty sure it was Milton Sorrell—goes by Milty. He runs a gun shop out of his barn on the outskirts of Rogersville. He's had several brushes with the law over the years."

"Ever convicted of anything?" Grant asked.

"Not that I know of."

"Well, I can check on that easy enough. Thanks for all your help, Mr. Addison, and for the lecture on the Barrett 50-Caliber. Awesome weapon."

"Wait, don't go quite yet," Addison said. "There's something else you need to hear."

Grant stopped and turned back to the gun smith with a questioning look on his face. "What's that?"

"One of the guys, not Milty, one of the others said that the deal had to be made by May first. He was kinda vague but he indicated that something big was gonna happen a day or two after that."

Grants interest peaked, "Did he say what it was?"

"No, but he did say that there was a whole lot of money involved and that he would be extremely displeased if the deal was not completed on time."

CHAPTER TWENTY-ONE

Thursday, April 16

WHEN GRANT GOT back to the office that afternoon Betsy Oppermann was sitting next to Bert's desk talking to the secretary. She immediately jumped up and rushed to Grant with a sob. They embraced and said nothing as they both wept. After a few moments she stepped back and looked him in the eyes. "Gideon, I don't understand how God could let something like this happen. Olga was such a wonderful person." Her voice choked as she continued, "I loved her so much—I just don't know how I'm going to get along without her. We had just found each other after that long separation…and now this."

Tears ran down Grant's face as he said, "I've had some of the same questions, Betsy. The only consolation I have is that Olga trusted the Lord Jesus as her Savior and I know for certain she's in heaven with him. You trusted Jesus that same day and now you've got to continue to trust him and cling to him."

"I'm trying to but it's so hard. If God is love and so powerful, why didn't he protect Olga? Why did he allow her to be killed?"

Bert was a woman of spiritual wisdom, a prayer warrior. She said, "Betsy, Sweetheart, the answers to these questions can come to us in only two ways. One, the Lord may choose, in His own time and way, to give you an answer from His Word and/or through His Spirit as you pray. Two, the answers may have to wait until we see Him face to face. Either way, we go on trusting the Lord, knowing He is too wise to ever make a mistake and too good and loving to ever be unkind."

Through her tears, Betsy said, "Thank you, Bert, I'll try to remember that."

As they were talking, June Whitlow slipped through the front door. She embraced Betsy and talked quietly to her for a few minutes while Grant and Bert watched in silence.

Bert, a faithful practitioner of ASAP, Always Say A Prayer, said, "Gather around, it's time to pray." They all joined hands and Bert led them to the Throne of Grace.

~~~~~

Major Dick Jenkins phoned Grant to inform him that the Medical Examiner had moved the autopsy of Olga to the top of his schedule and her body had been sent to Decker Funeral Home. The ME confirmed what the police and Grant believed to be the cause of death—exsanguination, severe loss of blood due to the gun shot to the neck which severed the carotid artery.

Grant passed that information on to those gathered in the office. Bert called the Decker Funeral Home and set an appointment for ten the next morning for the funeral arrangements to be made. Grant called Joe Bob Rounds and his Transitional Pastor. They all agreed to the set time.
~~~~~

~~~~~

On Friday morning, Sergeant Phil Early's wife, Beth Anne, met them at the entrance to the funeral home and led them into a conference room. She gently led them through the necessary paper work, the obituary for the newspaper, selection of a garment, a burial plot next to Olga's sister, Ingrid, and the most difficult part of the process, the selection of a casket. Joe Bob had been left well off financially at the death of his attorney mother so he wrote a check to cover the entire cost of the funeral and burial. Betsy, confused and distraught, only spoke in answer to questions directed to her. Pastor Jack Wallace spoke quietly to her, encouraging her to trust the Lord for strength and comfort.

The date and time of Olga's funeral was set for the next Monday, 10:00 a.m. at Highland Baptist Church, with Reverend Jack Wallace officiating.

"Brother Wallace," Grant said to the pastor, "thank you for being with us. This is such a hard time for all of us. Please keep us in your prayers."

"I assure you that the whole Highland Baptist family is praying for you all."

~~~~~

Grant took them all to lunch at Ziggies, and then he, Betsy and Joe Bob drove to the offices of Perkins, Perkins and Rounds Law Firm for the reading of Olga's last will and testament. Orsen Perkins, the senior partner of the firm, met them in one of the ornate conference rooms. He warmly greeted Gideon, in spite of the fact that it was Grant who had recently been responsible for Orsen's son, Mason, going to prison for life. It was the first time Orsen had met Betsy and Joe Bob, the niece and nephew of his former law partner, the late Ingrid Oppermann Rounds.

Olga's will was uncomplicated. She left her partnership in the Grant and Oppermann Investigations agency to Gideon Grant. All her other possessions including her house, the log cabin on the Gasconade River, SUV and money were bequeathed to her cousin and best friend, Betsy Oppermann. Betsy sat in open mouthed amazement as Orsen told her the value of the property and the amount of money in the several accounts she now owned.

~~~~~

As they drove toward the office on Battlefield Road Grant said, "Betsy, you've got two weeks leave, and Joe Bob, you said the sheriff has given you a couple weeks' time off. How would you two like to help me find the person responsible for Olga's murder?"

Joe Bob said, "I was hoping you would ask that. Count me in."

"I don't know what I can do," Betsy said, "but I'll do anything you suggest that will help. We must find the man who shot her. He might be able to give us some information that would lead to whoever hired him."

"Yeah," Grant said, "that would help, but we'll have to work with what we have. I've got a couple of leads to follow up on."

"You're the pro, just tell us what to do," Joe Bob said.
~~~~~

Chapter Twenty-Two

Friday, April 17

GIDEON GRANT HAD always worked with a partner as a SPD detective and as a private investigator and he liked it that way. He didn't say anything about it to either Betsy or Joe Bob but in the back of his mind he was wondering if he should approach one of them with the idea of becoming his newest partner. *This will bear some close watching and a whole lot of praying.*

Betsy had to do some paperwork transferring the title of Olga's house to her name so while she was doing that Grant and Joe Bob Rounds drove in separate vehicles to visit Attorney Maury Spooner.

Spooner's secretary was dressed and made up like an over aged hooker. When Grant and Joe Bob entered the office she laid a paperback novel on her desk and said, "Yeah, what can I do for you two?"

Grant handed her one of his cards and said, "My name is Gideon Grant and this is Deputy Robert Rounds. We'd like to see Mr. Spooner, please."

"Do you have an appointment with Mr. Spooner?" She asked as she popped her gum.

Grant looked around the office as if to say, "Why would we need an appointment? No one else is here." He said, "Just tell him we want to talk to him about Gregory Bando."

She picked up her phone and punched the intercom button. "Mau…uh, Mr. Spooner, a PI named Grant and a deputy sheriff want to talk to you."

"Tell them to call for an appointment next week. I'm busy now," Spooner said.

"They said they want to talk to you about a man named Gregory Bando. Do you know that guy?"

The silence with which they were greeted was deafening. After a couple minutes the secretary looked up at them with raised eye brows and shrugged.

Spooner sat at his desk with his head in his hands trying to think. *What do these guys know and how did they come to know it? What do I tell them? All I can do is deny any knowledge or connection to Bando. I'm an expert a bluffing so I'll do what I'm good at.* He punched the intercom button and said, "Send them in."

Spooner showed most of his teeth as he smiled broadly and said, "How can I help you gentlemen today? Have a seat," he said waving at chairs in front of his cluttered desk. He looked across the desk at the chairs and noticed that they were piled high with file folders. "Excuse me," he said with a chuckle, "I'll move that stuff." He came around the desk and piled the folders on the floor along with others already there.

When they were all seated Grant came straight to the point. "Spooner, there's a dead hit man in the morgue with connections to you. My partner is there also and it wouldn't surprise me to find that you're connected to that as well. I will find out what those connections are, count on it. You can make it a whole lot easier on yourself and everyone involved if you come clean about it now."

"Who do you think you are?" Spooner blustered. "You can't come in here and make those kinds of accusations. I'll sue you for defamation of character."

"From what I hear your character is way beyond defamation," Grant said with a quiet but chilling voice.

"I don't know what you're talking about, and neither do you. Now, get out of my office before I call the cops and have you arrested for harassment."

Grant stood and placed his hands on Spooner's desk and leaned into his face. "Little man, if haven't noticed, Deputy Rounds here is a *cop*. And if you think this is harassment, you ain't seen nothin' yet. As you well know, one of the victims of these hit men was my partner, my friend. You better believe I will find every person involved in her murder and bring them to justice—or worse."

Spooner leaned back in his chair almost falling over backward. His face was white as the blood drained from it and he felt as though he might faint. Weakly and slowly he said, "Get out of my office and leave me alone."

As Grant and Joe Bob walked out of Spooner's office Joe Bob stopped at his secretary's desk and said, "You might want to start looking for another job, Honey. I don't think this one will be available much longer."

The secretary had heard every word spoken in Spooner's office and her face registered pure panic as Grant and Rounds left.

~~~~~

As they exited the building onto Commercial Street Grant said, "All right, you wanted to help with this case."

"Absolutely. You bet."

"Okay, your job right now is to keep a watch on Lawyer Spooner and keep a record of everywhere he goes and everyone he talks to. I'm sure you can handle that."

Joe Bob smiled and said, "A piece of cake. I'll call you when he goes to bed."

"Sounds like a plan. See you later."
~~~~~

Chapter Twenty-Three

Friday, April 17

TWENTY MINUTES AFTER Grant and Rounds left Spooner's office the lawyer walked out and got into his Mercedes. He made an illegal U turn on Commercial Street and headed east. Joe Bob turned the key in the ignition of his much loved five year old Mustang and eased in behind Spooner about two cars back.

An hour and forty minutes later he followed Spooner to the gate of the state prison near Licking. He pulled his cell phone off his belt, looked at Gideon Grant's business card and dialed his number. Grant answered on the second ring. "Gideon Grant."

"Gideon, Joe Bob here. I followed Spooner out to the state pen at Licking. Do you have any idea who he'd be visiting out here?"

"Oh yeah, I'm pretty sure who it'd be. Three felons that Olga and I put away last year; Bella Dubois-Barnes, Scott Ireland and George Sumtner, are all incarcerated there. My guess would be that he's seeing either Ireland or Dubois since they're the more aggressive of the bunch. Sumtner is a follower. Without a doubt, Bella is the most vicious and vengeful of the bunch."

"What do you want me to do now?" Rounds asked.

"Come on back to town. Since Spooner's an attorney we'll have to go through official channels to find out for sure who he visited there. I'll ask Dick Jenkins to look into it for us. Good job, Joe Bob."

"Thanks; see you later."

~~~~~

As soon as the call from Rounds ended Grant called Major Dick Jenkins' direct line at SPD Headquarters on Chestnut Street. Jenkins' caller ID told him who was calling so he said, "Hello, Gideon, what's going on?"

Grant explained the Spooner incident to Jenkins and its possible connection to the attack on him and the murder of Olga. He then asked Jenkins to do whatever necessary to identify exactly who Spooner was visiting at South Central Correctional Center.

"That will be no problem. Attorney/client privilege applies to *what* is said, not to *who* says it. I'll get back to you soon."

"Thanks a lot," Grant said. *Now maybe we're getting somewhere on this mess.*

~~~~~

Grant was doing the never ending paperwork when Jenkins called back. "It was Bella Dubois-Barnes." Jenkins told him. "Spooner's been seeing her regularly for about three months. I'll have Sergeant Early bring him in for questioning, but first, as soon as I get a warrant, I'll have my computer-whiz sergeant do a little research on Mr. Spooners' bank account."

"Sounds like a good idea. Please call me as soon as you know anything."

~~~~~

Shortly after his conversation with Jenkins, Betsy came in the office. She was torn between the mixed emotions of losing her best friend and becoming a wealthy woman at the same time. She sat in a chair next to Bert's desk and poured her heart out to her. Bert quoted Romans 8:28 to her: "We know that in all things God works for the good of those who love him, who have been called according to his purpose." Then she said, "Both you and Olga are God's children through faith in Jesus. He loved Olga and he loves you. Now you have to trust him to know what he's doing in your life, and that he is always guided by his love, goodness and infinite wisdom. As his child and his servant, you are responsible to use what he has given you for his purposes and his glory."

Grant, who had been standing in the door to his office listening, said, "Amen, very well said, Bert. That helps me, too."

Bert blushed and said, "If anything *good* was said give the praise to the Lord."

Grant told the two women what had transpired with Maury Spooner and his connection to Dubois. "Major Jenkins is taking over from here. They're checking Spooners financials and then they'll take him in for questioning. Sergeant Phil Early is like a bulldog on a bone when he interrogates suspects. Spooner is in for a rough time."

"Sounds like it couldn't happen to a more deserving guy," Bert said.
~~~~~

CHAPTER TWENTY-FOUR

Friday, April 17

"**THIS TETRAZZINI IS** great, Mom." Grant said.

"Just wait 'til you taste the gooseberry cobbler," his mother Mildred replied.

June looked across the table in the older Grants dining room and said, "You're spoiling Gideon, Mrs. Grant; fixing his favorites."

"That's what moms do, Dear. And please, call me Mildred."

This was their first meal in the new home of Boyd and Mildred. She had gone all out to impress her future daughter-in-law. The table was set with her finest tablecloth and napkins, her mother's old and expensive china and silverware.

Gideon's father, Boyd, was a man of few words but he asked, "How're the wedding plans coming along?"

Gideon said, "That's June and Mom's department. I'm just along for the ride."

"Oh, Gideon Aaron Grant, you know better than that," Mildred said as she shook her finger at her second son.

June laughed and said, "We've got about two months to go and we're right on schedule. Everything's shaping up beautifully. Flowers and cake are ordered and paid for. Brides maid's dresses and being made already. I just have to find the right dress."

"How are the men folk shaping up," Mildred asked.

"As you know, Dick Jenkins is going to give me a way and your older son, Greg, will be Gideon's best man, so we're in good shape there."

"And," Mildred said with a gleam in her eyes, "my grandchildren are going to be flower girl and ring bearer."

"They are great kids," Gideon said with pride in his niece and nephew.

"Have you made your honeymoon plans yet?" Mildred asked.

"Now that's something I am into making plans about," Grant said leering at June gleefully.

"Now Gideon, don't you embarrass this nice girl," Boyd said. "If he's ever mean to you, June, just let me know. I can still take him down a notch or two."

"He's always a perfect gentleman," June said, "just like his mother taught him."

"No credit for the old man, eh?" said Boyd.

They all moved from the dining room to the den. A large stone fireplace was the main feature of the room, along with large, comfortable leather furniture, and a very large screen television.

Over coffee in the den the conversation turned to what was on everyone's mind, the murder of Olga Oppermann. Gideon told them all that had happened to date and assured them that those responsible would certainly be brought to justice.

Mildred looked at June and asked, "Is there any chance that you would prosecute the people who had Olga killed?"

"Probably not; it would be nearly impossible for me to be impartial in this case. I was a close friend to Olga so it would be unethical for me to prosecute the case. Even if it was offered to me, which is highly doubtful, I would have to recuse myself from it."

"Son," Boyd said, "do you have any idea who's after you?"

"We have a very good lead about the guy that got into the condo and the

person behind Olga's murder. But I really can't say much about it until the SPD detectives finish their investigation."

"What about that mess down in Nixa?" Mildred asked. "Do you have any idea who tried to frame you for killing that politician?"

"As far as we can tell, that's a totally different matter. The Nixa PD is working on it. Hopefully they'll wrap it up before too long."

Mildred sighed and said, "Sometimes I think it was easier to be way out in Arizona than so close. We didn't know about all this murder and mayhem then. One thing for sure, it's sure strengthened our prayer life."

CHAPTER TWENTY-FIVE

Saturday, April 18

BETSY OPPERMANN'S INSTRUCTIONS were to maintain visual contact with Milton Sorrell but under no circumstances was she to approach him. She found a spot on a high hill that overlooked Sorrell's barn/shop and observed the place through a pair of binoculars Grant provided. The afternoon weather was sunny and pleasant, so she had rolled down the windows on the new Mercury Marquis Olga had bought for her.

She admired the beauty of the Ozarks. Many of the surrounding hills and valleys had been cleared of timber and turned into lush, green pastureland. Cattle were in abundance and she recalled a Scripture passage that said that God owned the cattle on a thousand hills. She didn't remember where it was in the Bible or what it meant, but she felt good that she knew about it. It was a completely new manner of thinking for the new Christian.

Movement at the door of Sorrell's barn brought her attention back to the task at hand. She watched Sorrell walk from the barn to a pickup parked in the shade of an oak tree and get in. She made a note of the time on the clipboard Grant had given her and let Sorrell get on the blacktopped road to determine his direction before she started the Merc's engine. Since he was headed in her direction she waited until he passed her location and then pulled in behind him at a discrete distance.

The rolling hills and curves in the road made it difficult to keep Sorrell in sight without following too closely. She watched him pull onto the parking lot of a bar on the edge of Rogersville, exit his truck and walk quickly into the bar.

As a working U.S. Army Military Policewoman, Betsy was very familiar with bars. However, since becoming a Christian the previous year, bars and their environment had become very unattractive to her.

Even out of uniform she walked through the door in full confidence of fulfilling her mission of discovering who Sorrell was meeting. She took a seat on a bar stool and ordered a beer which she had no intention of drinking. The mirror behind the bar gave Betsy a clear view of Sorrell and the man who shared a booth across the room. Whereas Sorrell's large belly barely fit in the booth, his companion was as fit and lean as an active athlete. Even from across the room Betsy sensed something sinister about the man. His full head of hair was coal black as were his eyebrows and neatly trimmed mustache and goatee. His mouth was set in a hard line and his cheeks were lined with creases.

Betsy removed her cell phone from her purse and punched the button for the camera function. She casually spun around on the bar stool as though surveying the room and snapped a picture of the two men so quickly that no one noticed. She paid for the beer and walked out leaving it on the bar.

Back in her car she made notes of where she was and what she had observed. She decided to wait for Sorrell and the other man to leave and follow the second man. About twenty minutes later they emerged from the bar and walked to their separate vehicles. She watched the second man drive from the parking lot in a black Humvee and was about to start up the Merc when a shadow fell across her car window. She was startled to look up into the scowling face of Milton Sorrell. He knocked on the window. Rather than rolling the window down Betsy opened the car door and stepped out. She stood about four inches taller than Sorrell. She stepped toward him and he backed away a couple steps. "You want something, Mister?"

"I thought I saw you following me back there on the road. What're you up to, Lady?"

"It's a free country. A *lady* can go anywhere she chooses."

"Well, *Lady,* let me give you a piece of advice. Stay away from me and don't be poking your nose into my business if you know what's good for you."

"As I said, it's a free country…"

Sorrell drew back his hand to take a swing at Betsy. She smiled and waited for it to come. As he swung a haymaker at her head she put her MP training to work by grabbing his arm and quickly twisting it behind his back. She spun him around and slammed him against the side of her car while pulling his arm higher up his back. He squealed and struggled to get free to no avail.

"You had enough, tough guy?"

"Okay, okay."

She released his arm and stepped back. Sorrell spun around to take another swing at her. Betsy easily ducked under his fist and threw a right cross to his jaw with all her considerable weight behind it. He fell back against her car and then dropped to the pavement unconscious.

Betsy looked down at him, tisked a couple times, got in her Merc and drove off in pursuit of the other man.

The black Humvee was easy to keep in sight as she followed it west on Highway 60 into Springfield. She was careful to stay back as far as possible and to keep several vehicles between her and her quarry. The Humvee turned north on Highway 65 and then west toward the center of town where it paused at a large door in what appeared to be an abandoned warehouse. The door rolled up and then down again as the Humvee disappeared inside. Betsy made a note of the location and time and turned south toward the offices of Grant and Oppermann Investigations.

CHAPTER TWENTY-SIX

Monday, April 20

THE SANCTUARY OF Highland Baptist Church was packed well before the 10:00 a.m. announced time for Olga Oppermann's funeral service. Gideon Grant, June Whitlow, Betsy Oppermann, Joseph Robert Rounds and Jimmy and Alberta Young crowded together on the second pew on the left side of the sanctuary. Directly behind them were Major Richard Jenkins, his daughter, Angel, and Sheriff Lee Michaels and Grant's parents, Boyd and Mildred. Many officers of the SPD and GCSD were present and, of course, there were many people who merely came out of morbid curiosity because Olga's murder was sensational news.

Colorful flower arrangements were arrayed in abundance across the front of the sanctuary. The casket was almost covered by red roses, Olga's favorite.

Following the reading of Olga's obituary, the reading of John 14:1-6 and Romans 8:26-30, Ellen Jenkins brought tears to many eyes as she sang "Find Us Faithful" and "The

Old Rugged Cross," Olga's favorite hymn.

Transitional Pastor Jack Wallace spoke of Olga's conversion to Christ and of her rapid growth in her faith. He assured everyone present that because of her faith in Christ Olga resided in heaven from the moment of her untimely death. He told of her telling Gideon about seeing angels as she was dying and how each believer could be assured of being transported into the presence of the Lord by his angels at death or the return of the Lord Jesus Christ.

In the rear of the sanctuary, Detective Sergeant Phil Early stood and discretely captured those attending the service on a small digital camcorder. He paid particular attention to some faces he recognized and some he didn't. It was common knowledge among law enforcement that killers often attended the funerals of their victims. As he turned the camcorder to his right he stopped on a familiar face he was surprised to find in church for any reason. *What's Maury Spooner doing here? I'm supposed to bring him in for questioning this week. I'll bet Gideon'll be interested to know about this.*

Spooner was surrounded by people but he appeared to be alone. When the service ended Spooner slipped out the rear door rather than joining in the line of people being ushered down the aisle to view the earthly remains of Olga Oppermann. Phil followed Spooner to his car and captured the car and license on the camcorder.

~~~~~

Following the grave side service Sergeant Early caught up with Gideon and June before they got into her SUV. After uttering greetings and condolences Early said, "Thought you might be interested to know that Maury Spooner was at the funeral."

Grant frowned and said, "You better know it. What would that sleaze bag be doing at Olga's funeral?"
~~~~~

"Who is Maury Spooner?" June asked. "And why does it matter that he was at the funeral?"

"He's a low-class ambulance chasing lawyer with a very questionable reputation," Grant said. "And as you know, people involved in murders often show up at the victims' funerals. Their motives vary from morbid curiosity to attempting to cast off suspicion by appearing to care about the victims or their families."

"I can't think of any logical reason for Spooner's being there," Early said. "I'm supposed to bring him in for questioning this week."

"I saw him in his office last week," Gideon said. "Do you think you could hold off questioning him 'til I get another shot at him?"

"Don't see why not; we're in no hurry."

"I appreciate it," Grant said. "I'll see him today or tomorrow and call you. Okay?"

~~~~~

Gideon decided to talk to Spooner as soon as possible. He arrived at his law office on Commercial Street shortly after 2:00 p.m. When he saw the shabby office he almost felt sorry for Spooner—almost but not quite. His bimbo secretary said, "Mr. Spooner called a few minutes ago and said that he would not be in for the rest of the day."

"Do you have any idea where he might be? I need to ask him some questions."

She made a failed attempt to smile provocatively and said, "No idea where he might be. Maybe I can help you."

"I doubt it, but thanks," Gideon said as he stood to leave. As he reached for the door he stopped and turned back to her, "Come to think of it, maybe you can. Do you know why Spooner visits a convicted murderer named Bella Dubois-Barnes at the state pen at Licking?"

"I got no idea. Didn't know he did. Maybe he
~~~~~

represented her in court or something."

"Something, that's for sure," Grant said as he stepped through the door.

The secretary sat staring at the door. *What's the little jerk up to now? Maybe I better take the advice of that cute deputy and look for another job. If Maury winds up going to jail I sure don't intend to go with him.*

CHAPTER TWENTY-SEVEN

Monday, April 20

BREAKING THE SPEED limit all the way from Springfield Maury Spooner barely made it to the South-Central Correctional Center in time to see his client. The Unit Supervisor was not happy about having to get Bella out of the dining hall. When she arrived at the interview room she exhibited no pleasure at seeing the dumpy lawyer.

"What do you want now?" she snarled.

"Sit down and listen," Spooner said sternly.

Dubois sat at the table across from Spooner and leaned back in her chair waiting for Spooner to carry the conversation.

"Grant and the cops are getting too nosy. If we're gonna move on Grant it's gotta be soon, the sooner the better, in fact."

"What's happened?" Bella asked in a flat voice.

Spooner related to his client Grant's visit to his office earlier in the day, at least what he knew of it from his secretaries' phone call.

"The *sooner* Grant is taken care of the sooner I can sleep at night. You got somebody that can do the job?"

"You let me worry about that. We still agreed on the hundred 'G's?"

"It'll be arranged by this time tomorrow. And Spooner, you do know that if you try to stiff me I will absolutely send somebody to get you, don't you?"

"Yeah, I figured you'd feel like that. But don't you worry about it; I'll take care of it and then I plan to retire somewhere far from here."

Bella stood and looked down at Spooner, "I'll be watching the news for word of your success. Don't keep me waiting too long."

~~~~~

Spooner's permit to carry a concealed weapon had been revoked several years ago but he still possessed an old .38 revolver he'd inherited from his father. Driving toward Springfield he began to develop a plan. *Why should I share part of the hundred grand with some dumbo hit man? Being a PI couldn't require much smarts so it shouldn't be too hard to take out Grant myself. Yeah, that's just what I'll do.*

~~~~~

The sun went down as he was driving to his house so Spooner didn't notice the vintage Mustang parked on the opposite side of the street and down a couple houses from his.

Joe Bob watched Spooner leave his Mercedes on the driveway and enter the house before he dialed Gideon's cell phone. "He's just got home. You want me to stay on him for a while longer?"

"Yeah. Give him an hour or so to see if he goes to meet

anyone else."

"You got it. Talk to you later."

~~~~~

About fifteen minutes later Spooner exited his house, got in his Mercedes. Joe Bob followed him east on Battlefield and soon realized that he was driving toward the condominium complex where Gideon lived. He pulled his cell phone from his belt and dialed Grant's number. "Joe Bob here; he's heading toward your condo."

"Okay, I'll watch for him. You stay with him 'til we know what he's up to."

Spooner drove through the open gate of the complex and drove slowly by Grant's condo. Joe Bob watched him as he left the complex and headed east toward Highway 65. He called Grant, "Spooner drove by your place like he was casing it and then headed east."

"Yeah, I saw him," Grant said. "Wonder what he has on his mind."

"Nothing good, that's for sure."
~~~~~

CHAPTER TWENTY-EIGHT

Tuesday, April 21

BELLA DUBOIS-BARNES lay on her bunk in Cell Block C reading when a Corrections Officer appeared in the cell door. "You got a visitor, Dubois. Come on," she said impatiently.

"Who is it?"

"How should I know? I'm not your secretary. Move it."

Bella followed the CO through several steel doors until they arrived at the visitors' center, a long narrow room with booths on one side designed with partitions on each side, heavy Plexiglas between the inmate and visitor and a telephone with which to communicate. Everything was painted battleship gray. She was startled to see Gideon Grant sitting on the other side of the glass partition. She turned to the CO and said, "I don't want to talk to that man. Take me back to my cell."

"Look, the Assistant Warden said for you to talk to the man. So talk to him."

"He's the reason I'm in here. I hate him more than death

itself!"

The CO forcibly turned Bella around to face Grant, "That's your problem. Now, if you know what's good for you, sit down, pick up the phone and talk to the man."

Grant watched all this with an amused look on his face. When she put the phone to her ear Grant said, "Long time no see, Bella. How're you doing?"

Bella proceeded to call Grant every foul name she could think of and finally said, "What do you want?"

"Just wanted you to know that we know about your visits with Maury Spooner."

"So what? What are you gonna do, have me put in jail?"

"When I get the necessary evidence, I plan to put you on death row for the murder of Olga Oppermann."

"Lots of luck with that, slime ball."

"Luck has nothing to do with it. The same kind of investigation that put you in here will get you moved to Potosi and death row."

"There is no evidence for you to find.

"Speaking of Spooner, I doubt the little shyster will fare too well when he's questioned by the police."

"I don't know who or what you're talking about."

Grant smiled, "Oh, you know *who* all right. We have the date and time of every visit Spooner had with you. And to save his hide I imagine he'll be more than glad to tell us what you talked about."

"You go take a flying leap…" Bella abruptly stood and called out, "I'm through here. Take me back to my cell."

Back on her bunk she broke into a sweat thinking. *How'm I going to handle this mess? I didn't think things could get any worse, but death row!*

~~~~~

Grant drove straight to Maury Spooner's office on Commercial Street. When he knocked on the office door he
~~~~~

was greeted with a soft, “Come in.” The mascara from the secretaries eyes had run down her cheeks and her nose was red from wiping it with a tissue. He felt sorry for her, in fact that was the only reason he came by the office.

He looked for a name plate on her desk but there was none. “I’m sorry, but I never did catch your name.”

She snuffled a little and said, “Its Doreen…Doreen Slocum.”

“I’m sorry to have to tell you this, but your boss is about to be in deep trouble. I’m pretty sure he’ll not only lose his attorney’s license; more than likely he’ll wind up going to prison.”

“The little dope; I kept telling him he was getting in too deep, but would he listen? Oh, no. He kept saying, ‘One more score and we’ll retire to some island.’”

“Do you know anything about his connection to a woman prison inmate named Bella Dubois-Barnes?”

Doreen looked surprised. “No, there’s never been a mention of that name in any of our correspondence or files. I’d have remembered. I read all the newspaper accounts of her arrest and trial.”

She looked up at Grant as the light dawned in her brain. “Wait a minute. You’re that PI…Grant. Right? You’re the one who solved the case of all those murders in Vietnam so many years ago.”

“Guilty as charged,” he said.

“Is there anything you can do to help Maury?”

“I’m sorry, Doreen, but I don’t want to help Maury. I don’t have any solid evidence yet, but it looks as if he was involved in the murder of my partner, Olga Oppermann. And if that proves to be the case I will do everything in my power to put Maury Spooner not only in prison, but on death row.”

Doreen began to sob and after a moment or two said, “I’ve wasted fifteen years of my life waiting on Maury, believing all his lies and doing his dirty work. Now I’ve got to start all over again somewhere."

"Do you have any family you can turn to for help?"

"Just my Grandma down in Arkansas, but she's in a nursing home. I got a brother, but last I heard he was in prison himself. Not much help there."

"Do you have a church you can turn to?" Grant asked gently.

She chuckled, "I haven't been to church since I was about twelve years old. Mama always saw to it that me and Drake, that's my brother, went to Sunday School and church. But she and Daddy both drowned when their pickup got swept away in a flood when I was twelve. Grandma raised us but she never went in for church and stuff."

"Do you have any spiritual beliefs, Doreen?"

"Oh, I believe in God and stuff like that if that's what you mean."

Grant paused to breathe a silent prayer and then asked, "To you who is Jesus Christ?"

"I don't rightly know. I guess he's the reason for Christmas and Easter, isn't he?"

"Do you believe in heaven and hell?" Grant asked softly.

"Well, I'd sure like to believe in heaven, but I hope there's no such place as hell."

"If you were to die today, where would you go?"

"Go?" Doreen said. "I guess I'd just go into the ground and that'd be it."

"Doreen, if what you are saying you believe was wrong, would you want to know it?"

Doreen looked past Grant at the corner of the room for a long moment before she answered. "Maybe, maybe not; but with Maury in trouble and me probably going to be out of a job, I don't want to think about it right now. Okay?"

Grant smiled and said, "Okay. But I'd really like to talk to you again about this sometime soon."

She gave a slight little smile, "Well, Okay. I never knew a PI who talked about Jesus before. Most of 'em I know are slime balls."

"Yeah, to be honest, a couple years ago I was one of the slime balls. But when I trusted Jesus as my Savior and Lord everything in my life radically changed—for the better."

She looked down at here desk for a moment and then said, "I'll think about it, okay?"

"Sure," Gideon said as he handed her one of his cards. "If you have any questions or want to talk about Jesus some more, call me."

As he left the lawyer's office he looked at his watch and thought; *I'm going to be late picking up June for dinner.*

CHAPTER TWENTY-NINE

Tuesday, April 21

"I'M SORRY THAT I'm late, Sweetheart," Gideon said as he assisted June's climb into his pickup.

"No problem. I know how busy you must be."

"You're sweet to understand."

"In a sense we're both in the same line of work—justice. And we both know that the pursuit of justice has no respect for the clock, or even the calendar for that matter. Any leads to—Boy, it really makes me so angry that I want to start swearing.... I was about to ask if you have any leads to Olga's killer."

"Nothing concrete, but I'm pretty sure that a lawyer named Maury Spooner is involved somehow?"

"What makes you think so?"

"He's been making regular visits to Bella Dubois-Barnes in the state prison at Licking. Of course, we don't know what they were talking about because of attorney-client confidentiality, but knowing the two of them makes me think it's nothing good. If I was a betting man I'd lay down good money that Spooner is Bella's go between to the hit men that came after me and the one who killed Olga."

"How sad."

Grant turned to her with a questioning look.

"I mean that it's sad that anyone intelligent enough to become an attorney would waste his life like that."

"From what I gather he was at the very bottom of his class at law school and he's been in trouble with the bar association a couple times. Barely has enough clients to scrape by. I really feel sorry for his secretary."

"What do you mean?"

"If her boss goes to prison she'll have to find a new job. I doubt she's very skilled at what she does. I tried to witness to her but she said she wanted to think about it. She's in a real mess."

"Maybe I could help her somehow."

"What do you have in mind?"

"I don't know right off hand, but I'll try to think of something."

Grant smiled at her and said, "That's just one more thing I love about you."

"What?"

"That you're willing to try to help someone you don't even know."

June looked at him for a moment and said, "You look like something's bothering you, Sweetheart."

He told her about his conversation with Roger Addison at his gun shop in Republic.

"And something else that might lead somewhere. Betsy followed Milton Sorrell and another man to a bar in Rogersville. We don't know yet who the other man was but she was able to snap a picture of him with her cell phone. We gave it to Dick Jenkins and he's going to look into it for us.

"But what has me really concerned," he said, "is the

possibility of these horrific sniper rifles falling into the wrong hands, and we've got less than two weeks to keep it from happening."

"Isn't the A.T.F. looking into it?"

"Not that I know of." He sighed and said, "I guess it's time I gave them a call."

They spent an hour walking through the Bass Pro Shop. June was enthralled with the many stuffed animals. "They look so real." Gideon's favorite part was the display of firearms of all types and ages. He pointed to a large rifle and said, "That's the actual rifle used by Tom Seleck in the movie Quiggly Down Under."

June enjoyed her first trip upstairs to Hemingways, a favorite eatery in the Ozarks.

CHAPTER THIRTY

Wednesday, April 22

"**WHAT'S NEXT?" ASKED** Joe Bob Rounds. He sat in front of Gideon Grant's desk with his cousin Betsy Oppermann. Each sipped hot coffee occasionally as they talked.

Gideon responded with, "We have at least three persons of interest that we need to check into; Milton Sorrell, Maury Spooner and the man Betsy tailed into town last Saturday." He picked up the phone from his desk, punched the intercom button and spoke to Bert when she picked up her end. "Bert, would you please call Dick Jenkins and ask if they've come up with an ID on the man Betsy photographed in the bar on Saturday?"

"I'm on it, Boss."

"Sorrell knows you only too well, Betsy, so Joe Bob, I want you to tail Milton Sorrell all day. Try to keep him from making you, but if he does stay with him anyway. Let's see what makes him tick."

"Betsy, you sit on the lawyer, Maury Spooner. His

office is upstairs on the north side of Commercial about a block east of the old fire station. He shouldn't be too hard to keep up with. You both have the clip boards and time and event sheets I gave you to keep a record of…." Bert interrupted him, "Boss, Major Jenkins on line one."

"Thanks for getting back to me so quick, Dick."

"Not a problem. I've got some info on the man in the picture you sent over. Name is Morgan Toulair most recently from Arizona, some place called Bisbee. He's known by the Phoenix PD. The LEOs in Arizona, including the FBI and the ATF are very interested in Mr. Toulair. They've been trying to nail him for running an operation dealing with drugs and guns. He's even suspected in a couple murder cases. So far nothing has stuck to him. There are no outstanding warrants out on him so they have no reason to question him."

"Do you know where he's staying in town?"

"Sorry, no, at least not yet. We're faxing his photo to most of the hotels and motels in the area with a request that they call us if he is registered. Of course, he's probably using a fake name."

"Okay. Thanks again, Dick. It helps to know who he is and a little about him."

"Well," Jenkins said, "be careful, he has the reputation for being nasty when cornered."

Gideon told Joe Bob and Betsy the gist of his conversation with Jenkins and that he would be checking into the movements of Morgan Toulair. "If either of you see Toulair anywhere call me immediately. Don't try to make contact with him, just call me." They left to fulfill their respective surveillance assignments.

Chapter Thirty-One

Wednesday, April 22

MAURY SPOONER SAT at the kitchen table in his apartment contemplating his assignment. He frowned as he took a drink of his cold coffee. *Which of the four people Bella listed should I take out? There're three women and one man. I'm not much of a gentleman but I can't help but wonder how I would feel if it was one of my three sisters. And one woman's already been killed. So I guess that leaves the man, Grant's father. Now, how do I go about doing this without getting caught?*

It had taken some effort to find the address of Boyd and Mildred Grant's home since they were recent arrivals. At 7:45 a.m. he parked across the street and three houses to the south of their house to watch. *He's retired so he may have some routine activities that will make it easier for me.*

Spooner sipped a cup of McDonald's coffee and waited. *For a hundred g's I can wait a long time if I have to.* His coffee was still hot when the front door of the Grant home opened and Boyd came out. He stood on the front porch and stretched. After a few minutes he ran down the sidewalk and on to the street right toward Spooner's car. Spooner grabbed a magazine from the passenger seat and held it up so that Boyd could not see his face. He need not have bothered since Boyd paid no attention to him or his car.

Spooner watched Boyd in his rear view mirror until he turned a corner to the right. He started the Mercedes, made a U turn and slowly followed Boyd staying far enough back that he would not be noticed—he hoped.

Boyd continued east on a street with no sidewalks running at a slow trot. After a few blocks he turned right again, continued to his street and made another right completing a circular route back to his house.

All right, he must make that little run every morning. That's one thing to keep in mind. He parked on the street again and took up his watch. After about an hour he went to sleep. He woke with a jerk and looked at his watch but since he didn't know what time he went to sleep he had no idea how long he slept. He swore at himself as he thought; *Now I don't know if he's at home or gone somewhere. I'm not cut out for this kind of stuff.*

He about jumped out of his skin when he heard a tapping on his window. He looked out to see Boyd Grant standing there with a grin on his face. Spooner turned on the ignition and rolled down the driver's side window.

"Thought I'd make it easier for you," Boyd said. "That is *if* you're following me. I'm headed over to the Price Cutter on east Battlefield. That way you won't loose me."

"Following you," Spooner sputtered. "Why would I be following you? I…I'm waiting for a client. I'm a lawyer, I don't *follow* people."

"Okay, have it your way. See you." Boyd went to his SUV and drove away.

Spooner sat in his car pounding on the steering wheel and swearing profusely at his inadequacy in stalking his quarry. *Maybe I should have gone after one of the women.*

Speaking of women, Spooner failed to see the large, blond woman sitting in a new Mercury watching him.

~~~~~

When Boyd returned home Spooner's Mercedes was gone. *I wonder who that guy was. Said he was a lawyer. Think I'll call Gideon and see what he thinks about it.*

"Describe him for me, Dad," Gideon said after Boyd had told him what happened.

"He was pretty heavy set, looked to be short—hard to tell with him setting in his car. His hair was combed over trying to hide his bald head."

"Yeah, I know exactly who he is. A scumbag lawyer named Maury Spooner. Betsy's trailing him as we speak. She was probably watching him follow you. She hasn't called in yet but I'm sure she will soon."

"Did I tell you that I talked to him, Son?"

"You what? What do you mean you talked to him?"

"Well I'd spotted him tailing me when I went for my run. Then I saw him parked just down the street from our house so I slipped up behind his car and knocked on his window." Boyd chuckled and said, "I think he may have wet his pants when I knocked on the window—really spooked him."

"What did you say to him?"

"Told him I was going to the Price Cutter on East Battlefield so that *if* he was following me he wouldn't loose me. He sputtered a bit and then said, 'I'm a lawyer; I don't follow people."

Gideon was laughing so hard tears ran down his cheeks. "Dad, you are too much! I love it."

"Well, the jerk'll think twice before he tries to follow me around."

"That's probably true. But there is a very serious side to
~~~~~

all this. I strongly suspect that Spooner is watching you so that he can figure out your routine movements so that he can have some hit man kill you."

"Kill *me*? Why would anyone want to kill me? I haven't harmed anyone that I know of."

"It's not you they're really after; it's me. I'm pretty sure that's why Olga was killed. Do you remember that woman bank vice president I helped send to prison last winter?"

"That Dubois woman? Sure—is she behind this?"

"I'm almost certain she is. Dad, I want you to stay close to the house 'til I get to the bottom of this. Olga's death is almost more than I can bear; I sure don't want anything to happen to you, or to Mom."

"I took care of myself in Nam and I can do it here, too."

"I know, Dad. Just be very careful, please."

~~~~~

Grant's cell phone rang. The caller ID indicated that Joe Bob Rounds was calling. "Yeah, Joe Bob, what's happening?"

"I just got a call from the office and I've got to be in court this afternoon. A case I worked on months ago just came up and I've got to testify."

"Not a problem. Been there, done that many times. Call me when you're free."

"I hate not being able to tail Sorrell for you."

"Not to worry. I don't have a clue as to where Toulair is so I'll go check on Sorrell."
~~~~~

CHAPTER THIRTY-TWO

Wednesday, April 22

LATER IN THE day when Bill Townsend failed to show up for his pay check at the usual time Sorrell became worried about his old friend and drove his pickup down to the hay field. A large goose necked trailer sat at the far edge of the field. Four round bales of hay sat on the trailer. A fifth was on the ground behind the trailer.

All five of those bales were on the trailer yesterday. Sorrell opened the gate to the field and drove across the new mown hay toward the trailer. As he dismounted his truck and walked toward the bale on the ground he saw a man's leg sticking out from under the bale.

He recognized Bill's boot and cried out, "Oh, man, Bill, what've you gone and done to yourself? I told you and told you to be careful down here."

Sorrell went to the bed of his pickup, took a heavy rope with a hook attached to it from the tool box. He sank the hook into the side of the bale furthest from his truck and tied the rope to the heavy chrome grill on the front. He got in, cranked up the engine and eased back slowly rolling the large bale from Bill's body.

As he looked at his old friend's body he failed to notice the strange angle at which his head lay. He pulled his cell phone from the pocket of his bib overalls and dialed 911.

Within an hour the Greene County Sheriff's Department, the Rogersville Volunteer Fire Department and the County Medical Examiner's Office had men on the scene of the *accident.* The ME, Dr. Arnold Lee, knelt to examine the body and then stood and faced Detective Deputy Cal Unger, the senior Sheriff's deputy on the scene. "I won't say for certain until I get him on the table, but unless I'm wrong, which as you know is a rare event, this man's neck was broken before the bale of hay fell on him."

"That would change this from the scene of an accident to a murder investigation and this entire field into a crime scene," said Unger with a frown. He groaned and said, "Just what I need, a hundred-acre crime scene to search."

"Don't jump the gun," said Dr. Lee. "So far it's only an educated guess."

"Well, since as you said, you are rarely wrong in cases like this, to be on the safe side this will be treated as a crime scene until you tell me differently."

~~~~~

On his way to see Milton Sorrell Gideon Grant saw the collection of emergency and sheriff's department vehicles on the side of the road and in the hay field. His old lawman curiosity wouldn't allow him to pass by until he learned what was going on. He stopped and exited his truck and walked across the lush green alfalfa toward the gathering by the trailer. A sheriff's deputy stopped him about twenty yards from the trailer and said, "Sorry, Mister, this is a crime scene. You can't go any further."

"I understand Deputy. I'm an ex-cop and know the
~~~~~

routine." He spotted Detective Deputy Cal Unger. "Look, Deputy, would you tell Detective Unger that Gideon Grant is here?" He gave the deputy one of his cards.

"Oh, okay," the deputy said as he looked at Grant's card and suddenly remembered where he's seen Grant's face—in the newspaper account of the murder of Olga Oppermann. "Sure, Mr. Grant. I'm real sorry about your partner gettin' killed."

"Thanks, Deputy. She was a really fine woman and a great partner."

The deputy sensed Grant's discomfort and said, "I'll go tell Detective Unger you're here."

Grant watched as the deputy approached Unger and spoke to him. Unger looked at Grant and waved for him to come on into the group.

"What's goin' on, Cal?" Grant asked as he drew to within a few yards of Unger and gazed at the body lying nearby.

"Not real sure yet; we've either got a tragic accident here, or as the ME suspects, a murder victim. He thinks the victim's neck was broken before the bale of hay was dropped on him."

Grant looked at the hay bale and asked, "How much does that thing weigh?"

"Mr. Sorrell there," Unger pointed at Milton Sorrell, "says somewhere in the neighborhood of a thousand pounds."

"Enough to do some serious damage if it fell on you," Grant said.

Grant turned to look at Sorrell. He leaned in toward Unger and asked in a low voice, "What can you tell me about Sorrell? He's the reason I'm out here in the boonies."

"Not much," Unger said. "He owns this hay field and the surrounding woods. Has a gun repair shop in the barn behind his house. Says he's lived here all his life—born here."

"Do you know if he has a record?"

"Don't have a clue. Haven't had a reason to check on it. Why?"

"Just curious."

"Does it have anything to do with your partner's death?"

"I doubt it; has to do with another matter I'm looking into," Grant said.

"Well, as you can see, I've got my hands full with this death right now, but if I can do anything to help later, let me know."

"Okay," Grant said. "Thanks a lot. Is it all right with you if I talk to Sorrell for a few minutes?"

"Fine with me—we're through with him for now."

Grant walked over to Milton Sorrell and held out his hand for a shake. Sorrell seemed reluctant to take his hand but he finally reached for Grant's hand and gave it a brief, weak shake. Grant said, "I'm sorry for the loss of your friend."

"Yeah, me too. We been buddies most of our lives."

Grant handed him one of his cards and said, "I'm Gideon Grant, a private investigator from Springfield. Are you all right to answer a few questions?"

"Depends on what they are."

"Fair enough." As usual Gideon decided to go for broke and go after Sorrell with no holds barred. "What do you know about Barrett 50 caliber Sniper Rifles?" Grant watched Sorrell's body language carefully.

The question caught Sorrell off guard and he sputtered and almost choked before he could pull himself together, which was just the reaction Grant was looking for. "Not much." Sorrell finally managed to say. "Just that they're mighty expensive; way to rich for my blood. Why do you ask?"

"Well, as a gunsmith you must be pretty knowledgeable about weapons and I was looking for an expert. But if you don't know about them I guess I'll have to ask someone else."

Sorrell's mind raced to figure where Grant's question was coming from. *What has this guy heard? Has Toulair talked to him? He's got to know something or he wouldn't be here asking about those Barretts.* "Mister," he said, "I run a little gun repair shop in my barn. My customers are mostly local farmers and sportsmen, and they don't go in for those kinds of weapons. That's way too much firepower for anything around here."

"Okay," Grant replied. "I was out this way so I thought I'd check with you. I've got a friend with the ATF; maybe she can help me. Thanks anyway." *He's a poor liar,* Grant thought.

Grant turned from Sorrell and walked back to Cal Unger. Checking to be sure he was out of Sorrell's ear shot he told Unger, "Cal, I strongly suspect Sorrell over there is involved in some illegal gun sales. You might be wise to talk to the Sheriff about it and maybe even the ATF."

"What kind of gun sales?"

"Ask the ATF about Barrett 50 caliber Sniper Rifles."

"50 cal… Good night," Unger said with raised eyebrows, "those things are huge—shoot accurately for about half a mile. What makes you think there's something like that goin' on 'round here?"

"Just some rumors goin' around," Grant said as he decided not to tell everything he'd heard yet. As he walked toward his pickup he thought, *Milton Sorrell will bear some watching.*

CHAPTER THIRTY-THREE

Thursday, April 23

MAURY SPOONER SAT back in his office chair and strained to think of a way to kill Boyd Grant and not get caught doing it. Okay, what have I got to use as a weapon? I've got the 38 revolver I inherited from Dad although it's not much of a gun and with the little three-inch barrel I'd have to get real close to hit anybody with it. He couldn't remember when the permit had expired.

I've got my car I could run over him but that'd probably damage the car and get blood and skin and stuff on it for the cops to find. I've to a kitchen full of sharp knives but that's really up close and way to personal. Nope, not a knife.

Maybe I ought to find another hit man and hire him to do it. No, I need all the money I can scrape together if I'm gonna be able to retire and leave the country. I've got to do both Grant's old man and then Grant himself. That'll set me up for good.

A smile slowly spread across his face as an idea began to form. "It's crazy, but maybe it's just crazy enough to work."

~~~~~

As Boyd Grant opened his front door following his morning run he heard the phone ringing. Mildred, he knew, left earlier to baby sit their new granddaughter. He grabbed up the receiver and said, "Hello."

"Mr. Grant, this is Tom Jones at the Price Cutter pharmacy. There's been a mix up with a couple of your prescriptions and we need you to come down and help us get it straightened up."

"What'd you say your name was? You're not our regular pharmacist."

"Tom Jones—I'm a temp pharmacy assistant."

"Oh, okay, I'll be there in about an hour. I've got to shower and eat a bite of breakfast before I come."

"That'll be perfect, Mr. Grant. We really appreciate it."

~~~~~

Boyd Grant was about two blocks from his house when he came to a stop sign at a cross street. A heavy set woman was standing with her hands on the sign as though was holding her up. Boyd was barely stopped when the woman collapsed to the ground on her stomach. Boyd put his SUV in park, jumped out and ran to see if he could assist her.

As he bent over to examine the woman she suddenly turned over and jammed a gun into Boyd's stomach. "Don't say a word, Grant," a man's voice said. "Just get back in your rig and keep your mouth shut and do exactly what I tell you to do. Got it?"

Boyd looked closer at the woman's face. "Why, you're that lawyer that was following me around. What are you up to now?"

"I told you to keep your mouth shut. Get in the truck or I'll shoot you right here and now."

"Okay, okay, just relax. I don't need a new belly button."

When Boyd belted himself in behind the steering wheel and Spooner parked himself in the passenger seat Boyd said, "Okay, now what?"

"Drive where I tell you to go and don't try any tricks or funny stuff."

They drove for about twenty minutes in silence. Spooner directed Boyd to stop at a boat ramp on Lake Springfield which was just south of town.

"What now?" Grant asked. "We goin' for a swim?"

"I hope you like the water, wise guy, 'cause you're goin' for a long swim." Spooner kept the pistol aimed at Boyd as he pulled a syringe from his coat pocket and removed the cover from the needle. "This way you won't feel a thing—no pain, no fear, no nothin'."

"If you think I'm going to let you stick that thing in me you've got another think coming. I rather be shot."

"Makes me no difference...." The passenger side door suddenly opened as Spooner pulled the trigger on his pistol. Spooner's hand jerked and everything went black for Boyd as the bullet grazed the back of Boyd Grant's head.

Betsy jerked Spooner out of the vehicle and slammed him down on the concrete loading ramp. She pulled the pistol from his right hand and commanded him to stay where he was.

Unconscious, Boyd's left foot slipped off the brake peddle and his right foot pressed the accelerator driving the SUV into the lake. Water quickly filled the vehicle as it sank. Betsy ran into the water and grabbed the back of the SUV in an attempt to stop its forward movement into deeper water but it was too heavy and the forward momentum too strong. She moved to reach the driver's side door and found the water so deep she was required to swim. She pulled on the door handle but it was locked. The water rose swiftly inside the SUV reaching Boyd's chest as he remained slumped over the steering wheel.

All Betsy training as a soldier and an MP came back to her. *Do not panic. You can do this. Get to the door on the other side and extract Mr. Grant.* She swam over the hood of the SUV to the open passenger door. By then the water reached Boyd's chin. Betsy sucked in a deep breath of air and ducked into the water inside the SUV. *Got to get the seat belt unfastened first.* That done she took hold of Boyd's shirt sleeve and began pulling him toward the open door. The SUV gave a sudden lurch and Betsy banged her head on the rear view mirror. Everything went black for a moment and she sucked in water. She nearly panicked when she couldn't get a breath.

Strong hands pulled her from the SUV which was totally submerged by then. Gideon pushed her to the surface where she gulped precious air and swam toward the shore. Seconds later he broke the surface pulling his father behind him. Revived by the water Boyd was able to swim ashore alongside his son.

After Gideon placed a pair of plastic handcuffs on the cowering lawyer he, Betsy and Boyd sat on the ground the catch their breath. "Thank God," Betsy said to Gideon, "that you came when I called you about Spooner grabbing your Dad."

~~~~~

When confronted with the evidence against him, Attorney Maury Spooner knew his best bet was to tell all. He was charged with the attempted murder of Boyd Grant, as an accomplice in the attempted murder of Gideon Grant and the murder of Olga Oppermann. He claimed that he knew nothing about the murder of Senator Gardner Burkes.
~~~~~

Bella Dubois-Barnes was placed in solitary confinement until her trial for the murder of Olga. Olga's killer, Byron Ledbetter, was discovered in a rundown motel on the west side of Springfield. The ME determined that he had bled to death.

One case closed.

CHAPTER THIRTY-FOUR

BERT SECURED A 10:30 a.m. appointment for Gideon with an ATF agent the next day. The office was located in the Federal Building on John Q. Hammons Parkway. It took several minutes to get through security before taking an elevator to the fourth-floor office.

A male receptionist was seated behind a mahogany desk about ten feet from the elevator door. He appeared to be in his mid-thirty's, very fit and wearing a dark suit, white shirt and blue tie. *Must be the ATF uniform,* he thought. As Grant approached the desk the man looked up from his computer and with a slight smile asked, "May I help you, Sir?"

"I hope so." He handed the man his card. "I have an appointment with Agent Sullivan at 10:30. Is he it??

The man smiled and said, *"She* is in and expecting you."

"Okay, I've got no problem at all with a lady agent."

The man pointed to his left and said, "Go down that hall to the last door on the left. I think the door is open."

"Thank you very much."

Grant approached the door, stopped and knocked gently

on the jamb.

A very female voice said, “Come in. You must be Mr. Grant.”

He entered and quickly surveyed the room. It was very governmental; nothing fancy but very functional. The lady stood behind her desk and reached her hand across it.

Grant reached to shake it discovering a very firm grip. The name plate on her desk identified her as AFT Agent Joyce Sullivan. She was tall for a woman; not quite six feet, slim as a long-distance runner. She wore very little make up and her coal black hair was cut short and curled.

“Thank you for seeing me,” Grant said. He sat in the chair she pointed at in front of the desk.

“Your reputation precedes you, Mr. Grant. Some of our FBI agents speak well of you.”

“That was a few years ago. They were very helpful...after we got over a few hurdles.”

“Well, we feds do have a reputation also, I'm afraid. So, what can I do for you?”

“I'm working on a case that may have some interest to the ATF. About a week ago State Senator Burkes called me about an investigation he wanted me to do for him.”

“The murdered Senator Burkes?”

“Yes, ma'am. In pursuing the matter I've run across information that the matter he wanted investigated was related to the smuggling of Barrett 50 caliber rifles into Mexico.”

“Are you leading up to a man called Morgan Toulair?”

“That's exactly where I'm going. So you folks are aware of this.”

“We are very aware of Mr Toulair. But so far we've not been able to learn very much about him and his activities. He is a very cautious and slippery man.”

“Did you know that he is here, in Springfield?”

“No, we did not know that. How do you know about it?”

“Did you see the news about the shooting on

Battlefield?"

"Yes, I saw it on the news. Why?"

"That was my office that was shot up and we're pretty sure Toulair is the shooter. Let me show you a picture and see if you recognize the man." He pulled out his cell phone and pulled up the photo Betsy had taken in the bar and sent to his phone.

Handing Sullivan the phone he watched as she put on some reading glasses and looked closely at the small screen. "Yes, that is absolutely Tourlare, and I know the man he's with, Milton Sorrell. We've had our eye on him for some time. So, are they working together?"

"There's no doubt they're acquainted, and probably working together. Another gun repairman overheard them discussing the Barretts at gun show at the fairgrounds a few weeks ago."

"Unfortunately, talking about Barretts is not illegal."

"Please tell me what you know and suspect about Toulair."

That took about half an hour. The conclusion of the discussion lead Gideon to the decision to make a trip to southeastern Arizona.

CHAPTER THIRTY-FIVE

Saturday, April 25, Tucson, Arizona

GIDEON GRANT DROVE from Tucson International Airport in a rented GMC Tahoe SUV. The map the rental agency provided indicated that Interstate 19 Business Route North would soon put him on I-10 South to Benson and then State Highway 90 to Bisbee.

Bisbee, population about 8,000, famous for its abandoned Lavender Pit Queen Mine was founded in 1880 and named for Judge DeWitt Bisbee, one of the founders.

Driving south on Highway 90, Grant was amazed at the bareness of the terrain and the variety of cactus plants he saw. He stopped in the old town of Tombstone and walked around the old town, watched a fake gunfight on the main street and briefly toured the ancient cemetery, Boot Hill.

The ATF office in Springfield informed Grant that Morgan Toulair lived on a highly secured compound west of Bisbee near the small town of Palominas. The southern border of his two thousand acres of desert paralleled the border between the USA and Mexico. The ATF *suspected* that Toulair ran a profitable drug and gun smuggling operation from his ranch but so far they had no solid proof. Grant, with the blessing of the Agent Sullivan and the local Agent in Charge, planned to find the evidence they needed and stop the transfer of the Barrett 50 caliber Sniper Rifles.

Bert, working on the internet, made reservations for Grant at the old Copper Queen Hotel in Bisbee. At an elevation of 5,490 feet the air was brisk as he got out of the rental about a block from the hotel which had no parking of its own.

As he walked up the steps to the entrance of the one-hundred-year-old plus hotel he thought, *I wonder if I'll run into one of the three resident ghosts.* He checked in and was led to an ancient elevator that took him to the third floor and his room. He was pleasantly surprised at the accommodations of the old place. It had been modernized without losing its old west charm.

Before leaving Springfield Grant spoke to the Cochise County Sheriff which to his surprise was a woman named Carlene Mosley. Reluctantly she agreed to see him at 9:00 am the next day, Saturday. After a shower and some clean clothes, he went down to the hotel dining room for supper, then tired from the trip he went to bed early wondering what kind of reception Sheriff Mosley would give him, and if she would be receptive to his plan to visit the Toulair compound.

~~~~~

Following the directions given to him by the hotel desk clerk Grant arrived at the Cochise County Sheriff's Department just south of Bisbee. It consisted of a cluster of adobe looking buildings at the end of Judd Drive surrounded by bare dirt, rocks and several species of cactus plants.
~~~~~

At 8:30 a.m. the sun was already hot so he looked for a shady place to park with no luck. As he entered the lobby of the building his attention was drawn to a series of photographs of Cochise County Sheriffs from the first, Johnny Harris Behan, 1881, to the current Sheriff Mosley, the only woman to who have served in the position. Grant was intrigued to read that Sheriff Behan, after the famous gunfight at the O.K. Corral on October 26, 1881, had arrested the legendary Earp brothers, Virgil, Wyatt and Morgan, and Doc Holliday for the murder of Billy Clanton and Tom and Frank McLaury. The judge decided that the Earps and Holliday were justified in the killings.

I wonder if Sheriff Mosley is a tough as her predecessors appear to have been. As he continued to look at the photo gallery he was surprised to note that one of the recent sheriffs also bore the name of Mosley. *I wonder how they are related.*

"Can I help you, Sir?" Grant was drawn from the photos by the question. He turned to see a young woman in uniform. Her name tag read "Deputy May Topper."

"Yes, please," Grant said smiling. He handed her one of his cards and said, "I'm Gideon Grant, a private investigator from Springfield, Missouri. I have a nine o'clock appointment with Sheriff Mosley."

Deputy Topper extended her hand to Grant and as they shook hands she said, "Welcome to Cochise County, Mr. Grant. I'll check to see if the Sheriff is available. Will you wait here, please?"

"Of course, and thank you, very much."

In about five minutes she returned and motioned to him to follow her. She led him to a door in the rear of the building and knocked. He heard a strong voice say, "Come in."

Deputy Topper said, "Sheriff, this is Mr. Gideon Grant, the PI from Missouri."

Sheriff Mosley stepped around her desk and offered her

hand to Grant. As they shook hands she had a tight smile on her face and he smiled broadly. "I'm very pleased to meet you, Sheriff," he said.

"Likewise, please be seated," she said pointing to pair of chairs in front of her desk.

She sure is small to be a sheriff in the wild west, he thought. She appeared to be about five feet four or five inches tall and slim. Her auburn-colored hair was stylishly cut short. *There's nothing small about the gun she carries,* taking note of the automatic pistol carried in a shoulder harness.

"What can I do for you, Mr. Grant?"

"Let me say that I'm impressed with your layout here. I didn't expect anything so elaborate. And your people that I've met are very professional. As an ex-cop I appreciate that."

"Thank you. We work very hard at being professional in our work. I have to confess that I knew about you're being a police officer in the past. When you called for the appointment, I had Crystal, my secretary, run a background check on you. You check out very well I'm happy to say. In fact, I spoke to your friend, Major Jenkins, and he couldn't have been more complimentary."

"He's my former partner and my best friend, apart from my fiancé, that is."

"I take it that you're not here on vacation—that you're investigating something."

"Yes, Ma'am." He told her of the events following the telephone call from Senator Gardner Burkes to the death of Bill Townsend and especially his concern that the Barrett 50 caliber rifles could wind up in the wrong hands. He choked up as he related the murder of Olga Oppermann.

"I'm sorry about the loss of your partner. That's always hard to take. My father and my first husband were both killed in the line of duty so I know how it is to lose someone close to you through violence. You never really get over it.”

“To get back to the reason for my being here,” Grant said. “Our information is that a man named Morgan Toulair has a ranch just west of here. We think that he’s the one responsible for the deaths of Senator Burkes and Bill Townsend, and that he is behind the purchase of the rifles.”

“I share your concern about those rifles. We sure don’t need drug smugglers shooting at us with those cannons. If they were sent over into Mexico the drug runners could shoot at us across the border and we couldn’t respond. Homeland Security has tied our hands in that matter,” she said in a bitter tone.

“What do you know about Toulair?” Grant asked.

“Not as much as I’d like to know. He pretty well stays on his ranch; it’s about two thousand acres of desert, mesquite and cactus. Not much good for running stock—too little water and forage. The biggest problem is that his land borders Mexico and he does everything he can to thwart our efforts to control that part of the border. We’ve no doubt he’s bringing in drugs but so far we have no proof.”

“How do you think he gets them off his ranch to his customers?”

“That’s easy. He has his own airplane so he flies them out at night. He must drop them from the air somewhere because the Feds have met his plane several times and searched it without a trace of drugs. And sometimes he just flies out of his little air strip and then returns without landing anywhere. But since there is so much area out there to cover we don’t have a clue where he drops the stuff.”

"Have you ever been on his ranch, Sheriff?"

"Yes, a couple of times…routine stuff. Didn't learn anything worthwhile."

"I hope you don't mind," Grant said, "but I plan to make a visit out there myself, an unannounced night-time visit."

"Why would you think I might mind?"

"It's your county and if I were in your place I'd want to know what's going on. I mainly wanted to give you a heads up just in case something happened to me out there. I'd like someone to know I'm there and expected to return."

"Like you might need to be rescued?"

"Well, I hope it wouldn't come to that, but as you know, things don't always go as planned."

"Just be very careful. The last thing I need is a dead out-of-state PI on my hands. Way too much paperwork," she said with a smile. She stood indicating that the meeting was over. Grant shook her hand, thanked her and took his leave.

CHAPTER THIRTY-SIX

Sunday, April 26

THE SUN WAS just rising over the mountains to the east of Bisbee behind Grant's rental as he drove west toward Morgan Toulair's ranch. It glistened off the snowcapped mountain off in the distance to the west. The pre-dawn air was very cool at the five thousand feet plus elevation. *I never knew there were so many kinds of cactus plants.*

His stomach was full from an early breakfast at the hotel. A thermos of hot coffee and a bag of food bars lay on the passenger seat. He headed west on Highway 92 out of Bisbee toward the small town of Palominas following the directions on the very detailed map of Cochise County Sheriff Mosley had given him. Just before entering the town he crossed the San Pedro River which held far more sand than water.

In the middle of Palominas he turned south on a dirt road which according to the map would lead him to Toulair's ranch. The road was well maintained, which *speaks of the importance of Toulair in these parts*, Grant thought.

There was no mistaking the boundary of the ranch. An eight-foot-high chain link fence with well-marked *No Trespassing* signs seemed to surround the place. The dirt road Grant traveled paralleled the fence. Inside the fence another dirt road ran close to the fence. *That must be for security patrols to use.* The road ended at a large gate on the east side of the ranch/compound. Three-foot-wide rock pillars stood on either side of the gate. A rusty metal cut out sign above the gate announced the "Toulair Ranch." Two heavy metal gates met in the center and CCTV cameras focused on the gates and the surrounding area.

Grant slowly turned his rental around while observing every detail of the security precautions of the Toulair ranch. The dirt road turned west at the northeast corner of the property and Grant turned with it. He continued to drive slowly looking for the most promising spot to get through or over the fence. *Thank you, Lord, that it isn't electrified.* After about a mile the road veered off to the north away from the boundary of the ranch. He followed it long enough to determine that it did not return to the ranch.

About a half mile from the corner of the fence Grant spotted a gully which ran under the fence. Efforts had been made to secure the spot. *I believe with a little digging in the sand I might get under there.* Watching the odometer on the rental he measured the distance from the corner of the fence to the gully. *I'll be driving without lights tonight so I have to know just how far to go.*

~~~~~

Grant drove slowly back north toward Palominas. *No need to kick up a big cloud of dust to advertise my presence, besides I've got all day. Getting toward noon and that big breakfast is about gone. I'll check out that hot dog*
~~~~~

place I saw on my way through town.

Jimmy's Hot Dog Company occupied a bright yellow building in the edge of Palominas. A pair of enormous evergreen trees stood to the left of the building overshadowing some tables and chairs for those wishing to eat out of doors. One of the tables sported a large yellow and red umbrella. An eight-foot hot dog on the roof gave the idea that the specialty of the house was hot dogs.

Grant parked his rental, let down the windows to keep the Arizona sun from making the car too much of an oven and got out. Cool air met him as he entered through a bright red door. A man behind the counter smiled and said, "Ha-dee. What can I get cha?"

Returning the smile Grant said, "Looks like you specialize in hot dogs and I happen to really like a good hot dog."

"Really good dogs is all we have here. What kind would you like?"

Grant looked at the menu on the wall and said, "I didn't know there were so many kinds of hot dogs. Tell you what, give me what you think is your best one. I'll trust the judgment of the expert."

"Being from Chicago, I'd have to recommend the "Chicago Special."

"Sounds great, give me two of 'em, I'm pretty hungry, and a large Coke," said Grant.

Grant was the only customer in the place so he decided to try and make use of the time. "As you can probably tell, I'm not from around here. Name's Gideon Grant from Springfield, Missouri." He reached his hand over the counter to shake the man's hand.

"Jimmy's my name, and obviously, hot dogs is my game, pleased to meet you, Gideon. What brings you all the way from Missouri to Palominas?"

Grant decided to be up front with him. "I'm a Private Investigator looking into the smuggling of some weapons into Mexico."

"Way too much of that kind of thing goin' on in my opinion. Hope you do some good."

"What can you tell me about the Toulair Ranch down south of here?"

"Fer one thing, it's only been Toulair's for about two years. Before that it belonged to a long-time family around here, the Davidsons. The old man died and his only heir was a daughter who didn't want to bother running it so she sold it to Toulair. Got top dollar I hear. She's living it up in Tucson."

"What's with the chain link fence around the place?" Grant asked.

"That's what everybody around here would like to know. Old man Davidson let people hunt on the place. Just had to ask permission. Don't think he ever turned any locals down. Real nice guy."

Grant took a bite of his hot dog and said, "This is great. You ever meet Toulair?"

"No way. I don't think anybody in Palominas has ever even seen him. Only way we know who owns the place is by that sign over the gate. We hear his airplane goin' in and out but that's about all we know about the man."

"You happen to know what kind of plane it is?"

"No, I don't know squat about planes. It has two motors and makes a lot'a noise if that helps. That's all I know."

"I don't suppose it matters. But thanks for the info, and the hot dogs—they were great. In fact, why don't you fix me a couple to go? They'll make a good supper."

~~~~~

Figuring he was in for a long night, Grant parked in a shady spot away from the road, moved the seat of the rental back as far as it would go, reclined the seat back and took a nap. The alarm on his cell phone woke him two hours later.
~~~~~

Feeling refreshed he got out and walked around a bit to get the kinks out of his legs and back.

Before he got back in the car he pulled out his cell phone and punched the speed dial number for June Whitlow, his beautiful fiancé back in Springfield. She answered on the first ring. "I was hoping you'd call, Sweetheart. How are things going in the great desert Southwest?"

"So far, so good. Found a great place to get a hot dog. Speaking of dogs, how's Bruno doing, or perhaps maybe I should ask, 'How're you doing dog sitting him?'"

"Bruno and I are doing just fine. He's a comfort to have around."

"Great. Listen, Doll, there's something I'd like you to do for me tonight."

"You know I'll do anything I can for you, love of my life."

He told her of his plan and what she could do to help.

~~~~~

Just before dark he ate the hot dogs Jimmy had prepared for him. Driving without lights he headed back to the road and turned toward Toulair's place. At the corner of the fence he turned right and began watching the odometer measuring the distance to the gully where he planned to go under the fence.

Using a flashlight, he'd purchased in Bisbee he found a piece of 1 x 4 lumber about three feet long. It made a decent tool for digging under the fence. The sandy soil made for easy digging and he soon scooped out a space under the fence large enough for him to slither under the chain link wires. The first thing he did when he stood erect was to check his .45 Sig Saur for dirt and he also ensured the extra batteries for the flashlight were in his jacket pocket. He then looked up into the clear night sky at the
~~~~~

stars and hoped he would remember his Boy Scout training about using the stars as a compass. He was amazed at how bright the stars were so far from any artificial light.

It sure would be nice if I knew where I was going and what I'm looking for. I'll head as straight south as I can and hope I find something before I get to the Mexican border. I don't want to turn into an illegal alien in reverse. Using the stars as his guide and the flashlight to keep from walking into the many cactus plants he made slow progress. The ground was rough and the mesquite was thick. He had to stoop over often to get past them.

A noise like a pig grunting caused him to stop and swing his light to the right. *What in the world is that?* It's eyes gleaming in the glare of the flashlight, a large wild bore stood staring at him. It stood about three feet high at its shoulders and appeared to weigh about two hundred pounds. Wicked looking tusks curled out of each side of its mouth.

Grant eased his .45 out of its holster. *I sure don't want to give myself away by firing my gun, but if that thing charges me I'll have to.* "Shoo hog," he said trying to sound calm as well as not loud enough to be heard by humans who may be nearby.

"Get away. Git!" He waved his arms and the light hoping to scare it away. For a long moment the hog stared at Grant as though trying to make up its simple mind whether to take him on or not. Grant breathed a sigh of relief when the hog turned and disappeared into the brush and cactus. He kept the .45 in his hand just in case it decided to come back and have a go at him.

He began his slow trek south again. He spotted a couple of rattlesnakes but, thankfully, they slithered away. His luminous watch indicated it was half past ten when he spotted some lights about a hundred yards off to his right. *Bingo.*

Moving toward the lights revealed that the lights were

on a small air strip. A building sat off to the side which Grant determined must be a hangar for the airplane Jimmy had described. As he drew closer he could see that the building was far larger than necessary to house the plane. *It looks to be some kind of warehouse as well.* As far as he could tell there was no one out and about near the air strip.

More lights could be seen a couple hundred yards beyond the air strip and elevated at least a hundred feet. *The house must be situated on a hill. Hangar and warehouse first then the house.*

Grant began a circuitous route around the end of the air strip in order to stay out of the range of the lights. The ground had been cleared of most of the cactus so he was able to make better time. He approached the hangar from the dark side and discovered two windows and one door in that wall. *I wonder if there is some kind of security system.*

The door, as he expected, was locked. He cautiously looked through one of the windows. The interior was dark. Using his flashlight he examined the window for any sign of electronic security attachments. *None that I can see, but that doesn't necessarily mean there are none. Here goes nothing.* Using his elbow to soften the noise he broke one of the windowpanes. Following the tinkle of glass falling to the floor inside he stood stock still listening and hoping that no one else heard the noise. After a while he realized that he was holding his breath. Attempting to breath normally he reached through the broken window for the latch, unlocked it and raised the window enough for him to climb through.

The hangar and warehouse was all one large room. His flashlight revealed the plane located in the front of the building facing the large doors. All around him in the rear of the building were stacks of boxes setting on pallets. What few labels he could see were printed in Spanish. Using the Swiss Army knife he always carried he opened one of the cardboard boxes. *Marijuana. Must be a ton of it.*

He moved to another stack of boxes and discovered what looked to be heroin. Beyond that was a stack of long wooden boxes. *Looks like a stash of weapons of some kind. My knife won't help here.*

Grant shined the light around the hangar in search of something to pry open one of the boxes. He spotted a workbench against the wall near the airplane. He made his way through the stacks to the bench where he found a pry bar. Returning to the wooden boxes he carefully and as quietly as possible pried off the top of one of the boxes. *A-K 47s. No telling how many there are. ATF will love finding this.*

After climbing back through the window he pulled it down and locked it. *No doubt the broken window will raise some eyebrows in the morning. Now to check out the house.* Staying the dark as much as possible he began working his way through trees and cactus in the direction of the house on the hill. About halfway to the house Grant encountered a deep ravine which was about twenty feet wide. His flashlight could barely illuminate the bottom. *Now what? There's gotta be a bridge or something to get across this thing.*

He walked along the edge of the ravine slowly stopping every few yards to watch and listen. *Can't afford to be surprised by some security people.* He traveled about fifty yards before he spotted a wooden bridge spanning the ravine. He was uncomfortable about the large number of large trees one either side of the bridge—great hiding places.

"Stop right where you are, Mister. I've got a shotgun aimed right at you and at this range I won't miss." The voice was calm and confident.

Grant raised his hands above his head and waited. He didn't have to wait long. From behind him a hand reached around and removed his Sig Saur from its holster. "Put your hands on the tree to your left and assume the position. I'm sure you know the *position.*"

He assumed the position with his hands high on the tree trunk and his feet spread wide behind him. The security guard patted him down searching for additional weapons. He missed the small .38 revolver in Grant's ankle holster.

"Now, why don't you tell me what you're doing skulking around here?"

"Would you believe that I got lost and I'm looking for directions back to town?" Grant asked.

His smart remark was rewarded with a vicious poke in the back with the barrel of the shotgun. "Don't try to be cute, I ain't in the mood. Start walking slow like across the bridge and up to the house. We'll see how *smart* you are with Mr. Toulair."

"You mean I get to finally meet the infamous Mr. Toulair?"

"Yeah, and believe me, it'll be your worst nightmare. Now, move." He punctuated his command by poking Grant in the back with the barrel of the shotgun.

As they walked across the bridge and up the incline toward the house Grant prayed silently. *Lord, you've gotten me out of many messes that I got myself into and now I'm praying that you get me out of this one.*

Grant walked up the steps to the porch followed by the shotgun toting guard. The guard said, "Knock on the door."

He knocked and waited for a response. "Yeah, what is it?" was the response.

The guard shouted, "Its Archie. I caught an intruder."

Heavy footsteps could be heard approaching the door followed by the noise of several locks being unfastened. The door swung toward the inside of the house revealing a large, scowling Morgan Toulair. Grant was propelled through the door by the barrel of the shotgun in his back.

The house was old and showed its age. The room Grant entered was large and sparsely furnished with masculine chairs, sofas and tables. The finish on the bare wood floor was long since worn away. No pictures hung on the walls. There was a total absence of any feminine touch.

Toulair drew back his ham of a fist and swung it a Grant's jaw. Grant saw it coming and pulled his head back just in time to make the haymaker miss. Surprised, Toulair called to two other men who were in the room. "Hold him."

The two men each grabbed one of Grant's arms and pulled his hands up behind his back. Toulair said, "Now, let's see who you are, wise guy." Grant could only turn his head to keep Toulair's fist from hitting him in the face. As it was, the blow felt like it tore off his left ear. He staggered in pain and saw bright lights before his eyes.

"That's just a sample of what's comin' for you unless you give me a real good reason not to beat you to death. Comprenda? Now, who are you and what are you doing on my ranch?"

Since they were sure to discover his ID in his wallet Grant saw no use in telling Toulair anything but the truth. "My name is Gideon Grant. I'm a private investigator from Springfield, Missouri. I'm working with the ATF to trace some illegal gun smuggling. And Sheriff Mosley knows I'm here and why."

"Oh, boo-hoo, the big bad girl sheriff scares me right down to the ground." With that remark Toulair slammed his fist into Grants mid-section knocking the breath out of him. It took a couple minutes for him to regain his breath. Toulair drew back again to hit Grant but was interrupted by the ringing of Grant's cell phone. "Unless I miss my guess, that'll be the sheriff calling. She likes to keep track of out of town PIs on her turf."

"Answer it," Toulair growled. "Put it on speaker so we all can hear."

Grant did as he was told. "This is Gideon Grant. You're on speaker."

They all listened to the female voice. "Mr. Toulair, this is Sheriff Mosley. I'm assuming you have Mr. Grant with you as an unwilling guest. So you listen very carefully because I'm only gonna say this once. If Mr. Grant doesn't walk out that steel gate of yours within the next ten minutes, I and about a dozen of my deputies will knock the gate open with our vehicles and come in to have a close look at your operations. Oh, did I forget to mention that a few ATF agents will be along for the ride and they'll really enjoy seeing you on your home turf. You got that?"

Red in the face with rage, Toulair clinched his large hands into fists and his jaw muscles into knots. *The last thing I need right now with all that merchandise in the hangar is a bunch of cops running around.* "Mr. Grant is here all right, Sheriff, but he's here willingly and doing just fine. Right, Grant?"

"I'm able to walk to the gate, Sheriff. Thanks for the timely call."

"I'm waiting, Mr. Toulair. You've got fifteen minutes. I suggest you use them wisely." The call was disconnected.

Frowning, Toulair said to his hired strong men, "Let him go." To Grant he said, "Don't ever let me see your face here on my ranch or any where else. You, my friend, are a dead man walking." His cold, dead eyes convinced Grant that he meant exactly what he said. Without a word in response, Grant walked out of the house, across the bridge and down the dirt road to the gate. As he approached the gate it swung open electronically. He turned left and hustled up the road toward the rental car.

When he was about a hundred yards from the gate he heard it open again and looking back he saw a pickup exit the gate and turn toward him. Knowing he could not outrun the truck, Grant moved to the side and the road and waited. “I wonder what this is all about,” he said to himself.

The late model Ford was covered with dust. It stopped in the middle of the road even with Grant. Grant recognized one of the men who had been in the house with Toulair.

He dismounted the pickup and walked to where Grant

stood waiting. He was about five feet eight inches tall with a wiry build. "You have given me a huge problem," he said to Grant.

Surprised by the statement, Grant replied, "I'm afraid I don't have a clue as to what you're talking about."

"Not surprised about that, Mr. Grant. You see, my name is Victor Clark and I'm an undercover ATF agent. It has taken me almost a year to work my way into Toulair's confidence. Your showing up now makes it more difficult for me to remain in his confidence and undercover."

"How so?" asked Grant.

"I was sent out here tonight to eliminate you…to kill you. So now you can see my problem. I can't kill you and if I don't I can't go back to Toulair's house."

"That is a problem, all right," Grant said. "There must be a way the two of us can solve the problem."

"You have something in mind?"

"What if I overpowered you and took your gun? We could make it look like we were in a fight and you lost. Could you go back under that scenario?"

"He wouldn't like it, but I think I could sell it if we make it look good."

"Where do you want me to hit you?" Grant asked.

"A black eye would help sell it." Clark said. "Not that I want somebody as big as you to hit me at all. But I don't want to blow my cover."

Grant hesitated and said, "Wait a minute before we get into that. I've got something important to ask you. I'm a fairly new Christian and my pastor led me to promise I'd try to witness for Jesus at every opportunity."

Clark smiled, "That's great. I'm a Christian, too. Don't get a chance to talk about it much with Toulair's bunch, but I was saved while serving in the Marine Corps years ago out at Camp Pendleton. A buddy of mine led me to Christ. I lost track of him but I've never forgotten him. Best thing that ever happened to me."

This is just great, thought Grant, *now I've got punch a brother in Christ.* "You ready to get this done?"

"No sense waitin'." Clark closed his eyes and said, "Have at it."

God forgive me, Grant prayed silently as he hit Clark as hard as he dared; enough to give him a real black eye but not hard enough to do any real damage.

"Ouch!" Clark cried. "Man, what I go through for this job. On days like this I wish was an accountant or something; anything besides being a cop."

Grant grimaced and said, "To make it look real you might ought to roll around in the dirt a bit."

Clark dropped to the ground and rolled over a few times. He sat up and hit himself in the mouth splitting his lower lip. "A little blood might help sell the story."

Grant said, "I'll be praying for you, Victor. Be careful."

"And you better be careful also. You better believe that you are on Toulair's hit list now."

CHAPTER THIRTY-SEVEN

Monday, April 27, 7:00 a.m.

"**FROM THE LOOKS** of your face it doesn't look like your little excursion went so well," said Sheriff Mosley.

"For a cup of coffee I'll tell you all about it."

"Deal. Have a seat, Grant and I'll have some coffee brought in."

Grant sat in one of the chairs in front of the sheriff's desk, sipped the hot coffee and told her the whole story including the undercover ATF agent.

"That sounds like probable cause for a search warrant and an invasion of Mr. Toulair's little kingdom," she said rubbing her hands together. "I've been so wanting to go out there for months."

~~~~~

At 1:00 p.m. Sheriff Mosley, standing her full five feet, four inches plus her boots, called to order a group of about
~~~~~

twenty-five men and women made up of every deputy she could afford to pull off their assigned duties, five ATF agents from Tucson and three Arizona State Police officers.

"First of all, I want to introduce the man who made all this task force possible. Meet Gideon Grant, a PI from Missouri."

Grant nodded to the group but said nothing.

"All right, Grant, please tell us what you discovered last night."

Once again, Gideon told the story omitting the wild hog since he figured they were all aware of them. At Mosley's insistence he described ATF Agent Victor Clark as well as he could hoping he would not be harmed,

The sheriff took the floor again. "Here's the plan. We all meet here at 6:30. Everyone is to wear a vest, no exceptions. We'll check weapons and load up taking as few vehicles as possible. We'll hit their gate at eight; should be plenty dark by then. I'd like to take them all alive but we'll do what we have to do. The main thing I want is for all of us to come back alive and unharmed. So, go get some rest and if you're into it, pray a lot. See you at 6:30."

As the group filled out she said, "Not you, Grant. Stay here a bit."

He looked down at her from a foot above her and with a slight grin said, "Yes, ma'am."

"Sit down," she said, "you give me a crick in my neck."

He sat.

"Normally I wouldn't let a civilian get within a mile an operation like this, but since you were dumb enough to go out there without any backup and you know the lay of the land, and you have the reputation from the SPD of being a savvy cop, I'm going to allow you to come along."

"I appreciate it," he said quietly.

"But you will do exactly what I tell you and only what I tell you. Got it."

"You are the boss, Sheriff."

"You better believe it, and don't forget it," she said without a trace of a smile.

~~~~~

Gideon went to the hotel and laid down to sleep for three hours. After his inner alarm woke him at a little after four he showered and went to the hotel restaurant for an early supper. Before he had opportunity to order, a large man he recognized as one of the ATF agents approached his and asked, "Mind if I join you?"

"Not at all, please pull up a chair."

"Name's Bostich. Your first time to Arizona?" the agent asked.

Grant nodded and said, "Except for a trip to the Grand Canyon when I was a teen ager."

"I'm originally from Arkansas. Different world out here. But I love it."

"I can see that it'd take some getting used to."

Changing the subject, Bostich asked. "Was Victor okay? I had no idea he was out there, just that he'd been out of sight for about a year. I hate undercover work."

"Other than a black eye and a split lip, he was fine when I saw him last, that and a bunch of dirt. Have you known him long?"

"Went through the academy together. Worked together for a couple years in New Mexico. Lost track of him after that. Good guy."

"Yeah, I found out he and I are brothers in Christ. How about you, Bostich, do you know Jesus as your Savior and Lord?"

"Funny you should ask. Victor was after me all time to "come to Jesus," as he called it. Six months ago I did just that. Best thing ever happened to me."

"It's been about three years for me, and you're right about it being the best thing that ever happened."
~~~~~

They finished their steaks about the same time and Bostich said, "Why don't you ride with me tonight? I'm senior ATF agent in this operation so I'll take my rig."

"Sounds good to me. I'll have to borrow a vest from the sheriff. Left mine at home."

~~~~~

At 6:30 sharp Sheriff Mosley shouted, "All right, everyone mount up. Grant, I understand you're riding with Agent Bostich. Right?"

"Yes, ma'am."

"And you can drop the ma'am stuff. I'm probably younger than you."

Grant grinned and said, "If you say so, ma'am."

"Get in the truck, you big jerk. And keep your head down. All I need is for a civilian to get hurt on my beat."

Gideon considered he'd pushed the "ma'ams" far enough and just nodded.

~~~~~

It was about fifteen miles to the small town of Palominas. Grant saw Jimmy standing the door of his yellow hot dog shop watching the parade go by. He was grateful that the sky was overcast bring darkness on a bit quicker. Sheriff Mosley, riding with her chief deputy, led the column of nine vehicles.

When she arrived at the steel gate she backed across the road in her SUV and squealed all four tires as she barreled into the gate. The lock on the gate didn't have a chance of stopping the heavy SUV. She went up the road toward the house with her foot heavy on the accelerator.

Bostich, Grant and another ATF agent were two cars behind her. Before any of the invading vehicles came to a stop they were drawing fire from the house.

A round burst through the windshield and hit Bostich in the neck showering Grant with glass and blood. The bullet killed Bostich instantly having severed his spine. The momentum of the big SUV carried them forward toward the ravine in front of the house. Bostich's dead foot remained heavy on the accelerator and the SUV plunged into the ravine. Air bags exploded into Bostich and Grant.

Stunned but unhurt, Grant struggled to get free from the air bag. When he was free he reached for Bostich to see how bad he was hit. Suddenly he was glad he and Bostich had spoken of the Lord and salvation because it was clear that his new friend was gone to Heaven. “Make him welcome, Olga!”

The gun fire went on for several minutes until a man shouted from the house. “Stop shootin'!” We've got wounded in here.”

Mosley's chief deputy spoke through a bullhorn. “Every one that can come out of the house with your hands behind your heads. Do it now!”

Six men walked out the front door and were quickly handcuffed and put in the back of vehicles. Two men were unable to walk out; one was dead and the other badly wounded. He was carried away in an ambulance which the sheriff had arranged o follow them just in case.

Sheriff Mosley called out, “Is everyone okay?”

Her chief deputy said, “All our people are fine.”

“Grant,” she shouted. “Where's Grant?”

Gideon crawled out of the ravine and stood in the light of one of the trucks. “I'm here, Sheriff. I'm fine but we've lost Agent Bostich.”

“Oh, no,” she said. 'Oh, no!. That was not supposed to happen.”

One of the other ATF agents said, “We all knew this was possible when we signed up. But that doesn't help a bit now.”

Grant said, “At least we know he's gone to Heaven. Told

me he trusted Jesus not long ago."

"Yeah," the agent said, "he told us about that. But I wonder how much help that will be to his wife and three daughters.

Suddenly everyone looked to the dark sky as the sound of an airplane roared above them. "Confound it," the sheriff said, "Toulair's getting away. From the sound of it he's heading south into Mexico. I'll call the Federalizes to watch out for him."

CHAPTER THIRTY-EIGHT

Tuesday, April 28

Magdalena, Hermosillo, Mexico

RED FACED WITH anger, cursing Gideon Grant and fighting a tough cross wind that stirred up so much dust he could hardly see the ground, Toulair searched for the small landing strip he often used just east of the City of Magdalena. There was no control tower at the strip, in fact there were only two buildings and a place to buy fuel. That and just a single, rough dirt strip.

Holding the yoke with one hand he punched a number on his cell phone. "Hola, Senior Toulair. What can I do for you this fine day?"

"Come to the air strip and pick us up. Me and two of my men will be landing there in a few minutes."

"It is a bad day for flying with all this wind, Compadra."

"Tell me about it. But some days there is no choice, and this was one of those days. Just be there as soon as you can. We need a ride to your place."

"Si, I will be there."

"See to it," growled Toulair.

Turning to the two men with him in the cockpit he said, "We'll stop here for some fuel and food, and then head up to Missouri tomorrow. I've got a big score to settle with that meddling PI. I've lost my entire operation on the ranch. He is a walking dead man!"

"We're with you, Boss. I can't wait to get him in my sights. That was my brother that was killed. I want his blood on my hands!"

Flying low Toulair was able to spot the air strip. After making a pass to insure it was clear of other aircraft or livestock, he turned into the wind and approached the strip. It was so rough he was concerned about damaging the landing gears but he coasted to a stop with no apparent problems.

One of his men said, "I hope I never have to go through that again."

He taxied over to the fuel dump and shut down the engines. Checking the fuel gauges he determined that after the short flight from his ranch he had enough remaining fuel to make it to his Missouri destination. Suffocating heat met him as he opened the cabin door and descended the stairs that had been shoved to his plane. An old, dusty SUV was parked nearby.

"Welcome to Mexico, Senior Toulair," a small man in an expensive suit and a black hat shouted in broken English. His broad grin revealed gaps where several teeth were missing. The remaining ones were stained yellow from a lifetime of dipping snuff.

"Will you be staying long?"

"Just tonight. We need a place to sleep, some food and tequila."

"I know some lovely senoritas that would love to keep you company."

"Gracias, amigo, not this time. We've got plans to make.

Is Amiel around?"

"No, Amiel has moved away from here."

Touloure growled displeasure, "He was supposed to help close the deal on the rifles. What made him leave?"

"Some gringo missionaries came to his casa and he got religion or something. He said he could no longer work with us; that it was not right. Anyway, about a month ago he loaded his family and stuff in his old truck and left."

"Where'd he go?"

"He did not say and I have not heard. He is just gone. And speaking of the rifles, when can we expect delivery?"

"I've had some unexpected delays and some large loses thanks to a nosy private investigator, a lady sheriff and the ATF. My next stop is the PI's neighborhood. He is history!"

CHAPTER THIRTY-NINE

Tuesday evening, April 28,

Springfield-Branson National Airport

GRANT WALKED QUICKLY by the TSA agent seated near the exit of the secure area into the waiting arms of June Whitlow. Gideon's parents were close behind and behind them was a KY3 TV reporter and camera man.

"Hey, guys, it's so good to see y'all," he said. 'I've only been gone a few days. What's all the hubbub?"

"You've been on the network news, Son," Grant's dad said proudly.

His mother grabbed him by the lapels of his jacket and said, "You told me you were going to be careful. But you got into a gun fight! What am I gonna do with you?"

Grant hugged her tightly and said, "Just keep on prayin' for me."

"The news said y'all got a lot of bad guys but the main one got away. How'd that happen?" Boyd Grant asked.

They were walking toward the baggage carousel as they talked. As Grant watched for his bag he said, “He had an airplane on his ranch and he took off as soon as the shooting started. Left all his men to face the music. They weren't any too happy about that. A couple of them are telling the sheriff and the ATF all about Toulair's operation. If he ever come's back to the states and is caught he'll be in a federal pen for a long, long time.”

~~~~~

Unknown to Gideon, Toulair was on his way back to the states, the State of Missouri and the City of Springfield, with vengeance hot on his mind.
~~~~~

CHAPTER FORTY

Wednesday, April 29

THAT EVENING GIDEON Grant, his fiancé and family were in prayer meeting at Highland Baptist Church expressing their gratitude for his safe homecoming. Grant gave a brief testimony in which he gave the glory to God for all His goodness.

On the edge of town, in an obscure motel, Morgan Toulair was drinking whiskey, cursing Gideon Grant and plotting ways to make him suffer. *Not only Grant, but somebody is going to pay for revealing the location of my place in Arizona.*

~~~~~

The next morning Grant was in his office with Joe Bob Rounds and his cousin, Betsy Oppermann. Bert Young was at her desk in the front office typing up Grant's report of the events in Arizona.

"Do you think Toulair will try to get at you again?" Joe
~~~~~

Bob asked Grant.

“Who knows what that mad man will do? But we need to be on guard as if we know he was going to try,” Grant said.

“What do we watch for?” Betsy asked.

“Hard to say. Just be aware of what's going on around you at all times. Until we know he is behind bars or dead, we need to be paranoid; always thinking that he is around the next corner.”

“That's gonna get old in a hurry,” said Joe Bob.

“Yeah, but necessary if we're going to get much older.”

The sound of breaking glass followed by that of automatic weapon fire and bullets slamming into the wall of the outer office had them all diving for the floor as quickly as possible. It was all over in a matter of seconds and Grant was jumping up and calling out to Bert. “Bert, are you all right? Were you hit?”

A quavering voice said, “I'm Okay, Boss. But my beautiful office is a wreck! When I get my hands on whoever did this, I'm going to strangle him!”

Gideon, Joe Bob and Betsy helped Bert to her feet and surveyed the damage. The windows across the front of the building were all shattered and the wall in the rear of the office was full of bullet holes. Broken glass was scattered all over the office floor. The glass of several pictures was lying on the floor. Bert's computer was totaled. And Bert was so angry that had she not been so in love with Jesus she would be cursing a blue streak.

“How dare they?” she shouted. “And in broad daylight!”

“Hope our insurance will cover all this mess,” Gideon moaned.

He pulled out his cell phone and dialed 911.

~~~~~

Two hours later, Sergeant Phil Early of the SPD told the
~~~~~

three detectives what they had learned so far. “Fifteen rounds of nine-millimeter bullets came through the front window and into the office wall. Two of the rounds wrecked Mrs. Young's computer.”

“Thank you, Lord, that Bert wasn't hit,” Grant said.

“Amen to that,” Bert said.

At that time, Jimmy Young, Bert's cop husband walked in. After hugging his wife he turned to Grant and said, “I'm beginning to wonder if it's safe for my wife to work with you guys. This is getting serious...deadly serious.”

“Yeah, Jimmy,” Grant said, “It is bad and may get worse.”

“Any idea who the shooter was?”

“More than likely it was a gun rummer we're looking at, Morgan Toulair.”

“Yeah, we got a bulletin on him last week. Supposed to be in Arizona, isn't he?”

“He was a few days ago when I ran into him...well, he ran into me...with his fists.”

Early said, “One round went through the wall and destroyed your coffee machine.”

“That does it,” Grant said, “now I'm really mad. That machine made really great coffee.”

Early laughed and continued, “We've talked to the neighboring businesses but it happened so fast none of them saw anything to report. They heard the gun fire but by the time they looked out it was all over. Two drivers stopped and both said that the shooter was in a large SUV. Evidently there were two people in the vehicle because the shooter was traveling east and used the passenger's side window. Of course, no one got a tag number.”

Grant frowned and said, “Looks like Toulair is in town and has a helper. Great, just great!”

June Whitlow, Grant's fiancé and a county assistant prosecuting attorney, was allowed to cross the crime scene line, and ran straight into Grant's arms. “We just heard at the office and it scared me to death! Darling, are you sure none of you were injured?" *Primarily meaning, are you hurt?*"

"We're all just fine. Just angry and frustrated."

"Do you think it was that Toulair fellow again?" she asked.

"Probably. He's the only one who has it in for me at the moment....as far as I know."

"What are you going to do now?"

"Do our best to find him and lock him up."

"Oh, Sweetheart, please be careful. He's vicious and doesn't care who gets hurt."

~~~~~

A little later, Major Dick Jenkins entered the office carrying a rifle case and handed it to Grant. "Looks to me that you could use some additional fire power."

"What's this?" Grant asked.

"My old deer rifle. It's stopped several big bucks and it'll sure stop a crazy man with an automatic weapon. The scope will give you a few hundred yards advantage."

"I can't carry that around with me," Grant said.

"Just keep it in your truck so it'll be handy if you need it."

"Do it, Gideon," June said. "It will make me feel better."

"Okay, and thanks, Dick. It's been a while since I fired a rifle. Always been a handgun person."

Jenkins said, "Take it out to the police range and fire enough rounds to get familiar with it."

Early was listening to the conversation and said, "I'm scheduled to fire for qualification tomorrow morning, Gideon. You can go with me."

"Sounds like a plan, what time?"

"I'm scheduled at 0700. That okay with you."

"Not a problem, and thanks."
~~~~~

Sergeant Early spoke up, “All right, listen up, everybody. This office is now a crime scene and you all have to clear out until the CSU guys go over it. Since no blood was shed, it shouldn't take too long. Grant, I'll call you as soon as it's clear.”

Grant said, “Bert, you may as well go home. I'll call you when we can get back in. Joe Bob and Betsy, you come with me to my place. We've got some work to do. And, Sweetheart,” he said to June as he enveloped her in a great hug, “thanks for coming over. I'll see you later.”

“Remember,” she said, “we're supposed to be at your folks' for supper and more wedding plans.”

Grant struck himself in the forehead, “Thank you for reminding me. With all that's been going on I'd completely forgotten that

CHAPTER FORTY-ONE

Thursday, April 3

THE SPD CRIME Scene Unit had finished their work in the Offices of Grant and Oppermann Investigations and released them to Gideon and company. Gideon, Joe Bob and Betsy were gathered in Grant's office with coffee and doughnuts.

Joe Bob brought up the question of the hour. "How do you propose that we go about finding Morgan Toulair, Gideon?"

"Let's start with the little we know. Betsy, you followed Toulair to that warehouse on the east side of town."

"Yes," she said. "But I didn't get a look inside."

"I'll be surprised if he is there now, but it's the only place I know to start. Are you both armed?"

"As a deputy sheriff I stay armed," Joe Bob said.

"As an MP I have a permit to carry, also."

"Okay. And we all have Kevlar vests so we're good to go. We'll each take our own vehicles in case we have to split up later. Bert," he called, "we're leaving now in an effort to find Toulair. How's your new computer doing?"

"It's doing just fine," Boss. "Since we were able to save the hard drive from to old one we lost nothing at all."

Grant noted that the glass company was nearing completion on the job of replacing the office windows. Painters were coming during the weekend to patch the bullet holes and paint.

~~~~~

They parked a block from the warehouse and watched it for half an hour to see if there was any activity there. They were in contact with each other via cell phone.

"Let's get closer," Grant said. "I doesn't look like anyone is there."

Of course, the door was fastened with a heavy pad lock. The windows were too high to look in while standing on the ground. The Springfield City Utilities had left some sawhorses around a repair site. Grant and Joe Bob dragged one over to the wall under a window. Being the tallest of the group, Gideon climbed on the sawhorse to take a look inside. He had to wipe the window with the side of his hand to remove the grime. There was little light inside making it difficult to see. There were two vehicles, a sedan and a pickup, on the far side of the building. A movement caught his eye and he called out.

"Betsy, call 911. There's a body in there!"

"Alive or dead," Joe Bob asked.

"He's moving a little, so he must still be alive. Tell the 911 operator this is an emergency."

Fifteen minutes later SPD had broken the lock and allowed EMT to get to the man on the floor. The officers knew Gideon and allowed him to approach the injured man.

"Did Toulair do this to you?" Grant asked.

The EMT looked at Grant and shook his head slightly as if to say, *He's not going to make it."* "He's lost a lot of
~~~~~

blood. Better be quick so we can get him out of here."

The man was barely breathing but he said, "Yeah, the sorry SOB said he didn't need me anymore and just shot me. I played dead or he would have finished me."

"Do you know where he's headed?" Grant asked.

With his last breath he said, "Airport..." And he was gone.

The SPD sergeant in charge said, "I'll call the airport and tell them to keep his plane on the ground."

Grant said, "Don't bother. He won't be at the Springfield-Branson Airport. They're on the lookout for his plane and would have reported it to SPD if he landed there. It has to be some out of the way strip with no control tower; could even be a cow pasture. He's long gone by now."

~~~~~

Toulair had indeed taken off in his plane, but he didn't go far. He landed on a strip just south of Mt. Vernon, about thirty miles west of Springfield. An SUV was waiting nearby with the keys under the floor mat. He placed a Barrett 50 caliber rifle on the back seat, covered it with a blanket and headed north toward Springfield.

Toulair grinned as he covered the rifle, "Sorrell finally came through with one, but one's not near enough."
~~~~~

CHAPTER FORTY-TWO

GRANT'S CELL PHONE rang at 11:15 on Friday morning, April 31. "Grant here."

"Gideon, this is Phil Early. A civilian spotted Toulair in the Price Cutter store on west Kearney, but by the time our unit arrived he was long gone. Guy gave us a good description. Enough to know that it was indeed Toulair."

"Thanks, Phil. It's good to know where he is. It'll make us that much more careful."

"Every cop in Southwest Missouri is on the lookout for him," Early said.

"Do you know what he's driving?" Grant asked.

"Yeah, a black Chevy Suburban; no tag number of course."

When Grant ended he call Joe Bob asked, "Should we get on the streets and look for him?"

"Not yet," Grant said. "We'll let the leos find him. There are dozens of them and only three of us."

"There's another matter we need to discuss: Which of you will be my new partner. Betsy, you are bound to the

Army for another year or so, so that leaves you out of the equation. Besides that, I know you have your heart set on the SPD."

"Yes," she said, "that is my dream and my goal."

"So, Joe Bob, have you given any more thought to leaving the sheriff's department and joining up with me?"

"I've been thinking of nothing else for days. And, yeah, I think I'd like that a lot."

"I had Mr. Perkins of your Mom's old law firm draw up a contract that would make you a full partner. Half of the agency income over expenses will be yours. From past experience that would mean about a fifteen percent increase over your Greene County paycheck."

"That'll be great, but as you know I don't need the money after what Mom did for me in her will."

"Good, I'll keep the money then," Grant said with a grin.

"Mom took good care of me financially, but she didn't raise a dummy."

"It'll be good to have the name of Rounds back on the letterhead," Grant said.

"*Grant and Rounds Investigations.*"

~~~~~

Later that day in the offices of Perkins, Perkins and Rounds, the contract was signed and notarized. Orsen Perkins had decided to retain the P P and R name of his law firm even though his son, the second Perkins was in prison thanks to Gideon Grant, and Ingrid Rounds had died attempting to kill Gideon in a showdown on a rainy night at their cabin on the Gasconade River.

Joe Bob Rounds went straight to the office of the Greene County Sheriff to resign from his position of deputy sheriff immediately. The sheriff accepted his resignation with regrets and gave him a warm letter of recommendation.

Back at the office of Grant and Rounds Investigations
~~~~~

Joe Bob told Grant, “I'll miss wearing a badge, but as long as I can carry a gun, I'll get over it.”

“It didn't take me long,” Grant said. “And as PIs we have a lot of freedom the sworn officers don't.”

“Okay, Boss, what do we do next about Toulair?”

Grant's answer was interrupted by Bert calling to tell him that Major Jenkins was on the phone for him.

“Hey, Dick, what 's goin' on?”

“A lot. Two Missouri Troopers cornered Toulair over in Douglas County.”

“What's he doing way over there? That's over eighty miles from here.”

“No idea,” Jenkins said.

“Did they get him?”

“Not hardly. Toulair's carrying some kind of cannon and he shot out both of their engines. Didn't hurt either Trooper but it destroyed the engines of both cars...one shot each!”

“I can tell you what weapon he was using; a Barrett 50 caliber semiautomatic sniper riffle.”

“Fifty caliber? None of our officers have that kind of firepower.”

“Toulair's been trying to smuggle them into Mexico to the drug cartels. They'll pay really big buck for them.”

“After hearing about those cruisers I can see why. Bullets went right through the engine blocks.”

“So where is Toulair now?” Grant asked.

“A volunteer fireman in the little community of Pontiac saw him go over into Arkansas on a dirt road so we've had to turn it over the Arkansas lawmen.”

When Jenkins ended the call, Gideon told Joe Bob, “Get saddled up, we're going hunting. Our cops may not be able to go into the Natural State but nothing says we can't.”

CHAPTER FORTY-THREE

IT TOOK GIDEON and Joe Bob a little over two yours to drive to Pontiac, a small lake community sitting on the border between Missouri and Arkansas. Since there was only one main road through the community they had no problem finding the volunteer fire station. Within minutes they were sitting at a table in the station kitchen drinking some strong Louisiana coffee. The short, stocky fireman with the Cajun accent and sporting a white beard was eager to help them.

After introductions, the fireman, Butch, said, "Yeah, I saw him go by here yesterday like a bat outta Hades. Guess he didn't know the pavement stops in about a half mile and the road turns into rough gravel at the Arkansas line. I imagine it slowed him down pretty quick."

"Where does the road lead," Gideon asked.

"Unless you really know your way around it dead ends at Bull Shoals Lake."

Joe Bob's eyes lit up with excitement, "So he could be trapped down there somewhere!"

"I reckon," said the fireman.

"We'll take a look around before we head back to Springfield," Gideon said.

"Springfield? We had an interim preacher at our church from Springfield for a while. Pretty good old boy."

"Then I take it that you are a Jesus follower. Joe Bob and I are, too."

"Oh, yeah, I got saved a long time ago down in Louisiana. Grew up down there."

"Thanks for your help, Chuck. We're gonna head down into Arkansas and have a look around" Gideon gave him one of his cards and said, "If you happen to seem him again, please call me on the cell number. And whatever you do, do not try to stop him or make any contact with him. He is armed to the teeth and very dangerous."

Butch said, "I may be short, but I ain't dumb."

~~~~~

Before leaving the fire station, Grant and Rounds checked their side arms and the rifle to be sure there were rounds in the chambers and ready to immediately fire. Grant wondered if Olga may have failed to do that and died because of it.

The road was rough but Gideon's truck handled it with no problem. The road was lined with thick forest on both sides. They came to several side roads which they followed until they ended at the edge of the lake. They came across several fishing resorts, some with comfortable looking cabins and others looked very rough. After following a dozen or so side roads there was no sign of Toulair's SUV.

They had just turned north heading back to the Missouri line when Grant's cell phone rang. "Gideon Grant here," he said.

"This is Butch at the fire station. That SUV just went by goin' north about as fast as he went south."

"Thanks, Butch. We're headed that way ourselves."
~~~~~

"There's a lot of ways he can go," Butch said. "Do you have any idea where he might be headed?"

"My guess is that he's headed back to Springfield. He has some unfinished business there; namely finding and killing me."

"Then his best route would be to go to Gainesville and take Highway 5 north. That's the quickest way to Springfield."

"We've got a Missouri map so we'll take that route, too. Thanks a lot."

~~~~~

On Highway 5 south of Gainesville they came on an Ozark County Sheriff's Deputy standing beside his car with the hood up. They pulled in behind him and stopped.

Gideon got out of his truck and said, "Can we help you in any way, Deputy?"

Wary of two strangers the deputy put his hand on his pistol. "First of all, who are you. I need to see some ID."

"Makes sense," Grant said. "I'm a PI from Springfield and this is my associate, Joe Bob Rounds. Until recently he was a Greene County Deputy."

They both held out their ID for the deputy's perusal.

"Okay, good. Some guy armed with a cannon just took out my engine. I pulled him over for speeding and before I got out of my unit he stepped out of his SUV and with one shot wrecked my engine. I dove for cover behind the unit and he took off."

"His name is Morgan Toulair. We've been after him for weeks. That gun you mentioned is indeed a cannon: a 50 caliber Barrett to be exact."

"I've been shootin' all my life but I never heard anything as loud as that thing. My ears are still ringin' Toulair you say; we got a bulletin on him. A bad'n."

"You're blessed that he shot your car and not you. Just
~~~~~

being winged by that Barrett would probably kill you."

"I'm glad my wife and my Mom pray for me all the time," he said. "The good Lord saved me again."

"Can we give you a ride anywhere?" Grant asked.

"Thanks, but no. I called the office and they're sending a deputy to get me and a wrecker for the unit. Gonna cost Ozark County a bundle to replace this engine. Bullet went all the way through it."

"Toulair's trying to smuggle them into Mexico and we are working with the AFT to stop him. So if we're going to do any good we've got to get a move on. God bless you, Deputy."

"I'll put out the word to our units and the State Patrol so they won't stop you for speeding."

"Thanks, that'll help a lot."

Grant's truck laid down rubber as they sped north.

~~~~~

Sweating bullets as he arrived at the small town of Gainesville the gunman said to himself, "I've got to change vehicles. That deputy will call and have an APB put out on me and this SUV."

He spotted a late model Chevy pick up parked by an out building of a small farm. He pulled his pistol from his holster as he drove up beside it and parked. He waited three or four minutes to see if anyone was home in the old house sitting about thirty yards from the truck. He dismounted the SUV and tried the doors of the pick up which were locked. Looking around for anyone who could see him and seeing no one, he picked up a softball size rock and smashed the driver's side window. He reached through and unlocked the door and climbed in. In less than three minutes he had hot wired the ignition and started the engine. He noted that the gas gauge indicated a half tank of fuel. Satisfied, he pulled the truck onto the highway and drove slowly through
~~~~~

Gainesville and got onto Highway 5 headed north.

The highway was smooth and the curves allowed speed up to seventy.

"Oh, no!" He shouted to himself as he spotted two sheriff's deputies' cars blocking the highway about a quarter mile in front of him. A side road off to the right had a sign which read "Caney Mountain Conservation Area."

He turned on the road thinking, "It's got to come out somewhere." He silently cursed his luck, the cops who blocked his way, and especially Gideon Grant.

CHAPTER FORTY-FOUR

GIDEON AND JOE Bob arrived about five minutes later and they, too, spotted the two deputies' cars blocking the highway. They pulled up to the cars, got out, showed their identification again.

"I'm fairly certain we're chasin' the guy you're looking for," Grant said. "He's driving a black Surburban. Has he been by here?"

"No," one of the deputies said. "We've been here for about two hours and the only vehicles have been locals and a few lake tourists."

Both of the car radios squawked and one of the deputies went to answer the call. After a couple minutes he returned and said, "Toulair got another ride and I think we just saw it turn on the Caney Mountain road. If it was him he's trapped himself 'cause that road dead ends on top of Caney Mountain.

Grant asked, "How far to the top of the mountain?'

"About five miles of rough road mostly up hill. Whole lot of rocks."

"Toulair's a killer. He's got to be stopped and this

appears to be a good place to do it," Grant said.

One of the deputies got on a cell phone and called the sheriff's office for instructions. When he ended the call he said, "The sheriff said for us to wait here for him and some more deputies. And he's calling for some state troopers to help."

Grant handed the deputy one of his cards, "Just in case we can help in any way call me."

The deputy looked doubtful but said, "Okay, thanks."

~~~~~

While Grant and the deputies waited for the sheriff and his "posse" the stolen pick-up reached the top of Caney Mountain and the driver discovered that the road stopped there. Furious, and cursing all the while, he turned the stolen truck around and started back down the mountain in the direction from which he had come. "Got to go easy or I could blow a tire on all these rocks.

"The law is sure to come looking for me up here," he said to himself. "Got to figure a way to get past them and back on the highway."

He came to a side road off to the right. He drove on it until the truck would be out of sight and stopped. He took the Barrett and walked back toward the road leading up the mountain. He walked back up the road toward the top of the mountain searching for a good ambush spot. The road, no more than a two track, passed between two large outcropping of rocks.

"That narrow gap will do." He unfolded the bi-pod stand attached to the rifle, laid down behind it and sighted it in on the gap in the rocks to wait.

~~~~~

Gideon and Joe Bob sat in Grant's truck and watched as

the sheriff led four units with two deputies each and two state trooper units down a dusty, rock strewn road with sirens blaring and lights flashing. The narrow road demanded they go single file. The drivers in the last few cars had to drop back in order to see because of the thick dust in the air. They soon had to slow down for some sharp turns and a low water crossing that caught the sheriff by surprise.

The sheriff arrived at the gap between the rock walls and without slowing down he passed through followed by the rest of the posse.

~~~~~

Watching through the rifle scope, the shooter took careful aim at the last car in the line. When it reached the gap he fired a 50 caliber round through the hood into the engine. The car immediately stopped and the state trooper jumped out and took cover behind the rock outcropping. He calmly placed an incendiary round in the breach and pumped it into the fuel tank of the patrol unit. The car exploded and burst into flames completely blocking the road. Car parts rained down on the area.

“I love it when a plan works out,” he said as he started running back to where he'd left the stolen truck.

~~~~~

Grant and Rounds heard the loud cracks of the Barrett followed by the explosion.

“Sounds like they've made contact with Toulair,” Grant said. “Hope they get him so we won't have to get involved.”

Just as he said that his cell phone rang. “Grant here.”

“This is Deputy Boyd. Toulair outsmarted us. He shot up the last car in the line and blocked the road so we can't get out 'til we move a burning car. He's coming your way!"

"Okay, we'll watch for him and try to stop him."

To Joe Bob he said, "We've got to find some substantial protection from that Barrett rifle. Vehicles wont help and most trees wont either. Gotta be big, hard rocks."

They mounted Grant's truck and started down the road in the direction the posse had taken. "Keep a sharp eye out. We don't want to be surprised by him."

"Look at that dust cloud coming our way. Gotta be him as fast as he's comin'."

"Not enough rocks here for good cover. There's a creek just ahead of us. We'll have to make it do."

Grant pulled the truck onto the concrete low water crossing and turned it side ways blocking the road.

"Hope he doesn't decide to shoot up my truck. Come on, let's get down behind the creek bank."

The Chevy truck stopped about fifty yards from the creek. Grant took careful aim with the Winchester and shot both front tires of the pickup.

"It's gonna stop here one way or another," he said.

The driver got out of the truck holding the Barrett. He shouted curses at Gideon and Joe Bob.'

"Give it up, Toulair," Grant shouted. "You're trapped between us and the sheriff and his deputies."

The driver aimed the Barrett at Grant and shouted, "We'll see how long that'll last. You can't hide from this weapon."

The Barrett roared but Grant and Rounds were down below the creek bank out of the line of fire. Dirt and rocks flew all over them as the 50 caliber rounds dug into the earth above them.

Grant handed the Winchester to Rounds and said, "You try to keep him pinned down where he is. I'm gonna go down the creek a ways and try to sneak around behind him. Be careful not to show yourself. He's a crack shot with that cannon. And keep praying."

"Good night, this water is freezin'. Doesn't matter, I've got to get around behind Toulair and that cannon." He came to a spot where the water was about waist deep. "Be a good swimming hole," he said as he waded across it. Rocks, fallen trees and limbs in the water made the going difficult at times. After he'd gone about a hundred yards he climbed out of the creek and began climbing up a steep hill that shielded him from the killer's line of vision. The hill was covered with loose rocks, cedars and scrub oaks. Shivering from the cold water, Grant literally crawled on his all fours up the hill.

"Got to stay low. That Barrett is way too powerful to take on with a handgun"

The gunman had been watching for such an action because as Grant topped the hill a fifty caliber round went through an eight inch oak within inches of his head. "Thank you, Lord, for that near miss!"

"I'm out of range with this pistol and I'm easily within his range. Got to flank him somehow."

Still crawling on his belly, Grant moved off to his right hiding behind every available rock. A rock the size of a basketball exploded into gravel as the Barrett roared.

Pieces of the rock pounded into Grant's bald head. Blood began running into his eyes blurring his vision. He crawled faster to a new spot behind a larger rock.

Sensing that Toulair's attention was on Grant, Joe Bob raised up and fired several shots at the killer making him dive for cover. That diversion enabled Grant to move down the hill through the trees and closer to Toulair.

The killer stood erect and took aim at Joe Bob. Grant, wishing he were closer, emptied his clip at Toulair as he fired running toward him. "Can't let him shoot at Joe Bob; not going to loose another partner!"

He rammed another clip into his Glock as he hid behind another boulder.

Dropping the Barrett the shooter grabbed his left leg

above the knee. Cursing he pulled a pistol from under his jacket and turned it toward Grant.

Seeing this movement, Joe Bob raised up and took careful aim. The Winchester cracked and a 30 caliber round in his shoulder dropped the shooter to the ground.

He was reaching for his pistol when Grant reached him and kicked it out of his reach. He then put a number twelve foot on his chest and said, "Gotch ya."

The words had hardly left his mouth when he looked down at his captive and said, "Oh, good night, who are you? I've met Toulair and you're not him!"

CHAPTER FORTY-FIVE

LOOKING UP AT Grant the would be killer said, "Yeah, and I remember you from that night on the ranch. We should've killed you then. You were lucky when the lady sheriff called."

"That lady sheriff was my fiancée calling from Missouri and you dummys fell for it."

"You can be sure Morgan Toulair hasn't forgot it. You, my friend, are a walking dead man."

"Well, I really don't think I'm your friend, and as far as being a walking dead man, the Bible says that my "times are in His hand." I wont be dying until God is through with me here."

"Do you really believe that hogwash?"

"Yeah, I actually do believe it. Come on, get up. The sheriff will want to talk to you. Why don't you make it easier on yourself and tell us where Toulair is?"

"You've got to be kidding. Nobody rats on Morgan Toulair and lives to tell about it. I wouldn't be safe even in prison."

As they were talking, the sheriff and several of his

deputies approached them with weapons in their hands. One of the deputies quickly handcuffed the prisoner. The sheriff said, “Good job, young man. Looks like you got him.”

“We got this one, Sheriff, but he’s not the one we’re looking for. He’s just one of Toulair’s hired hands. Toulair is in the wind.”

“Well,” he sheriff drawled, “this one’s goin’ to jail for a long time. He shot at lawmen, destroyed at least two of our vehicles and stole another one.”

Grant said, “If you check with Arizona I imagine you’ll find they have several charges against him.”

“The more the better,” replied the sheriff. “I’ve called for an ambulance to take him to the nearest hospital up in Ava. I’ll have a deputy with him at all times.”

Grant shook hands with the sheriff and said, “You’re welcome to him. I’ve got to get back to Springfield and try to pick up some lead on his boss. He is a menace to society and he has sworn to kill me. And I am really offended by that.”

~~~~~

It was well after dark by the time Grant and Joe Bob drove the ninety miles back to his office on Battlefield Road. He called Dick Jenkins at home.

Jenkins said, “Sounds like you and Joe Bob have been busy down in Ozark County.”

“How’d you hear about it already?”

“With today’s internet and social media nothing that big stays secret for long.”

“Thankfully now one was hurt; except the bad guy that Joe Bob shot.”

“Bad buy? It wasn’t Toulair?”

“No, just one of his cronies. We thought we had him, but no such luck.”
~~~~~

"So," Jenkins said, "we've 'til got one of the worst killers still loose in the Ozarks."

"I'm afraid so. Joe Bob and I will focus one hundred per cent on finding him as soon as possible. As I'm sure you and all SPD are also."

"There's an all-state APB out on him. Hoped we would be able to cancel it when we thought you'd got him. But not yet."

Grant said, "I've got to let you go now and call June. She'll be worried sick."

"Good idea," Jenkins said, "give her my love."

~~~~~

Noticing the caller ID, June answered her phone on the first ring. "Gideon, are you all right, Darling? I was so scared when I saw it on the news."

"Thank you for caring so much, Babe. With you and so many others praying for me I was quite safe. And, as I told someone else today, my times are in God's good hands."

"And for that I am eternally grateful," she said. "What now?"

"Right now I've got to call Mom and Dad and then go get some sleep. First thing tomorrow we start a diligent search for Morgan Toulair."

"Please be careful, Gideon. I'm too young to be an almost bride. I love you so much."
~~~~~

CHAPTER FORTY-SIX

Friday, June 1, 8:15 a.m.

AFTER GIVING A full report to Bert Young, Gideon and Joe Bob settled at Grant's desk with coffee. "Are we back to square one, Boss?" Joe Bob asked.

"Hopefully not that far back. We can be fairly sure that Toulair is still in the area. The State Troopers found his airplane and have grounded it. It helps a lot to know he can't jump in it and go most anywhere quickly."

"I wonder if he has any of his men with him, and if so, how many?" Joe Bob said.

"None, I hope. Toulair's enough to handle by himself."

~~~~~

But Toulair was not alone. In the company of his last hired gun, an American Indian named George Bearclaw, he was in an old barn in the woods off Interstate 44 about fifty miles south of St. Louis. Scrub oak, maple and a few pine
~~~~~

trees made up the thick woods around them.

Toulair asked, "Are you sure this is the place he was to meet us?"

"Yeah, Boss. He said be in this barn at 0' ten hundred hours today."

"Well, it's almost noon and there's no sight of him so far. I'm about out of patience. This wait is gonna cost him big time."

Bearclaw stepped away from Toulair wanting as much distance between him and the boss as possible. He knew that failure could be deadly around Toulair.

"And he said he had ten Baretts to sell? Toulair asked.

"Yeah, Boss," Bearclaw replied with a bit of quaver in his voice.

"Do you have any idea how many people he'll have with him?"

"No, not a clue. What does it matter?"

"It matters because I don't have the cash to pay for those rifles. We're gonna have to high jack them."

"If you say so, Boss." But Bearclaw was very uncomfortable at the prospect of more gun play.

"We'll give it another half hour then we're out of here," Toulair said.

~~~~~

It was ten minutes later when a large white SUV approached the barn. When it stopped, Toulair and Bearclaw watched through a dirty window as three men exited the van. It was easy to see that under their light jackets they were armed. It was also easy to see which of the three was in charge. A man with gray hair gave instructions to two younger men who stayed back of him.

"This should be no problem if we take them by surprise," Toulair whispered.

The three men jumped in surprise when Toulair opened
~~~~~

the door and shouted, "I guess you know you're over two hours late, Blockheads!"

The leader reached under his jacket for his gun, but he was way to late as he was looking down the barrel of Toulair's weapon.

"Don't even think of it," Toulair warned.

The two younger men raised their hands in surrender.

"That's much better. Now lets see what you have for me."

"Look, Mister," said the gray-haired man, "we're not looking for any trouble;

just a simple sale. Our guns for your money. Just that simple."

"I really wish it was that simple. You see, my ranch was raided by the law a few days ago and with that I lost most of my cash. Not that I own you an explanation."

Before the man could respond, in rapid fire Toulair shot all three men in the chest. As the gun smoke cleared away he calmly told Bearclaw to open the van and check out the guns.

Carefully stepping around the three bodies the Indian went to the rear of the van only to find it was locked. Stepping to the driver's door he found the keys in the ignition.

As he removed the keys he spotted a wad of cash lying on the console between the seats.

Looking around to insure Toulair was not watching, he slipped the cash into his pocket.

Opening the rear door of the van they found ten wooden crates each about six feet long. Behind those crates was a truck size box full of 50 caliber ammunition. Dragging them out one at a time they used a tire iron to open each one. Toulair inspected each rifle to insure it was in working order.

"Alright, let's get 'em loaded in our rig," he told Bearclaw.

They had to fold the third and middle seats down to accommodate the crates.

They covered them with a tarpaulin.

"You get under the wheel and drive," Toulair told Bearclaw. "And drive very carefully. The last thing we need is to have some cop pull us over. It would be death for him and trouble for us and I don't need any more trouble."

Chapter Forty-Seven

SEVEN HOURS OF driving just under the speed limit brought them to a different warehouse just east of Springfield. Toulair had arranged for it earlier as a backup. He knew from past experience that the best laid plans can be fouled up.

"The cops have got my plane so I've got to figure a way to get these guns to Mexico. That's the only way I can get back on top with some money."

"We could drive them to the border," Bearclaw said, "but I don't see how we could ever get them across the border."

"That'd be way to risky. I've got to get someone from down there to fly up here and transport them and us back to Mexico."

"How long will that take?"

"Just long enough for me to take care of some other business right here in Springfield. I'm not leaving until that PI Grant is in a permanent horizontal position."

~~~~~
~~~~~

The next morning, Bearclaw, following orders from Toulair, was watching the offices of Grant and Rounds Investigations. He was located about a block from their office and on the other side of the street. They didn't think Grant had seen the Indian so it wouldn't matter if he spotted him watching. If Grant left the office Bearclaw was to follow him and report his location to Toulair.

Bearclaw didn't know that Grant parked in the rear of their building so he was surprised when Grant drove past him heading west on Battlefield Road. He had to hustle to get to his rental car before Grant got out of sight. He followed him to Highland Baptist Church and watched him meet a woman in the parking lot and together walk into the church. He called Toulair on his cell to report.

"Boss, he just went into a church. He had a woman with him."

Toulair asked, "Where is it? Give me an address or some directions."

"The sign says, Highland Baptist Church. I think this is Bostonian Street. Don't see any number on the building."

"That's enough for GPS to get me there. George. Keep watch and I'll be there as soon as I can drive across town."

~~~~~

In the pastor's study, Gideon and June were being given some wise counsel about marriage by their new pastor, Matthew Clarkson.

"To sum it all up," the pastor said, "a successful marriage must be centered on a mutual commitment to the Lord Jesus Christ. The closer you each are to Jesus, the closer you will be to each other."

"Thank you, Brother Matthew," June replied. "Thankfully, Gideon and I are in total agreement with that wonderful truth."
~~~~~

They all three stood and Gideon reached to shake the pastor's hand. He didn't get to shake his hand because a 50 caliber bullet slammed into the wall behind them. Gideon immediately dragged June and the pastor to the floor.

"Whatever you do, stay down," he commanded. "That has to be Toulair!"

"Toulair?" The pastor asked. "Who's Toulair?"

"He's a heartless killer. We've been chasing each other for weeks."

"Each other? What do you mean?, asked the pastor.

"First I chased him out of Arizona and now he's here trying to chase me out of Springfield, or to be more accurate, out of this world."

"Grant, can you hear me?" shouted Toulair. "That was just a warning shot. I've got a lady in my sights through an office window."

"What do you want, Toulair?" Shouted Grant.

"I want you to come out here so we can take a little ride."

"Gideon," June said in desperation, "you can't go out there; he'll kill you!"

"If I don't he'll kill Mrs. Sills. I can't let that happen. Besides, if he wanted to kill me he could have done it with that shot."

Grant drew June into a hug and whispered in her ear, "Pray for me. It'll be alright. It has to be, I've got a wedding to go to." He kissed her softly and stood.

"Okay, Toulair, I'm coming out. Hold your fire." He shouted.

"The whole church will be praying for you soon," Clarkson said.

"Thank you, and thank the folks for me."

Gideon walked to the office door and slowly opened it. He held is Glock in his right hand so Toulair could see it and then gently laid it down on the sidewalk by the door hopping that Toulair would leave it alone. *I don't want to have to buy another gun.*

Toulair and a man Gideon failed to recognize were standing by a large black SUV. Toulair had a Barrett 50 caliber rifle resting on the hood aimed at the church office. George Bearclaw held a large caliber revolver in his hand aimed at Grant.

"Come over here," commanded Toulair.

Grant slowly walked to the two armed men. Bearclaw put his revolver in his pocket and removed a pair of plastic hand cuffs from his pocket.

"Turn around and put your hands together."

As Grant obeyed, his hands were securely bound together.

"Now," Toulair said, "you get in the front passenger seat. George, you drive and I'll keep him covered from the back seat."

"Where to, Boss?"

"That little airport on the east side of town where they've got my plane impounded."

"But it'll be surrounded by cops," complained Bearclaw.

"Let me take care of that. Reach over and take Grant's cell phone from his pocket and hand it back to me."

~~~~~

June Whitlow was on the church office phone talking to Police Major Dick Jenkins. "That man Toulair fired a shot through the church office and demanded Gideon to go with him. They're in a big black SUV. I couldn't see the tag number. We don't know where they are going."

"We'll get an immediate APB out on it," Jenkins promised. "I know you're praying. Keep it up."

~~~~~

As Jenkins hung up from speaking to June, his private

phone rang. He saw that the call was from Grant, but figured it was anything but good news.

"Major Jenkins, here," he said.

"Well, Major whoever you are, listen closely. I know you're tight with that nosy PI Grant. I have him with me in handcuffs. I really want to shoot him, but I have a deal to make with you for his life."

"And what would that be?" Jenkins asked.

"Simple. I want my plane released, refueled and ready for take off ASAP."

Jenkins thought, *If he get's off the ground with Gideon, he's as good as dead.*

"Why should I believe you won't kill Grant even if we allow to fly away?"

"Just know that I will surely kill him if I don't get my plane, and get it soon."

Jenkins sighed and said, "I'll make arrangements for it."

Toulair roared, "If there's anyone on my plane, Grant dies! If there is anything wrong with my plane, Grant dies! If you try to get me with a sniper, Grant dies!"

"I get the message, Toulair."

Toulair said, "There's a cop car behind me! Call him off now, or Grant dies."

Jenkins nodded to a sergeant standing by and the instructions were radioed to the officer in pursuit to cease immediately.

Bearclaw was driving east on Division Street toward the old Springfield Airport when about a dozen SPD and State Trooper cars surrounded the SUV. He stopped and looked at Toulair for instructions.

Toulair, still on the cell phone with Major Jenkins said, "All right, Major wise guy, if you want Grant to see another day get all these cops and their cars out of my way, NOW!"

After a few minutes the cars moved to make a way for the SUV to go through the airport gate. Bearclaw saw

Toulair's plane and drove toward it.

"Get up as close to the door as possible," Toulair said. "Grant and I will make a quick transfer."

Doing as he was told, Bearclaw stopped just two feet from the stairs leading up to the fuselage. Toulair said, "Grant, you get out and stand on the first step. I'll be right behind you so don't do anything stupid."

"You've got the gun, you call the shots," Grant said.

George Bearclaw walked around the front of the SUV toward the stairs but Toulair aimed his pistol at him and said, "No, you stay here, George. I don't need you anymore."

"You dirty rat," Bearclaw hissed, "just shoot me. They'll lock me up and throw away the key."

"Them's the breaks," sneered Toulair.

Bearclaw threw up his hands and walked toward the waiting police officers.

Toulair stood close enough to Grant to cause any snipers to think twice about taking a shot. Upon entering the plane, Toulair quickly slammed the door closed and locked it. He told Grant to sit in one of the four seats in the front of the fuselage. Keeping his gun aimed at his heart he reached for a roll of duct tape.

Gideon bunched up his leg muscles to attack Toulair, but before could act, Toulair hit him in the head with his gun and everything went black.

CHAPTER FORTY-EIGHT

WHEN GIDEON WOKE up he found that he was bound to the seat with several rounds of duct tape, and he had a terrific headache. He also felt the vibrations of the plane and realized they were in the air. He presumed they were heading south toward Mexico.

The cockpit door opened and Toulair stepped out. "I see that you're over the little nap I gave you."

Grant just stared at him knowing any reply would be futile.

"Automatic pilot is a wonderful thing," he said as he sat next to Grant.

"If you're wondering why you're still alive," Toulair said with a menacing smile, "it's cause I don't want any blood on my plane floor, and I really want to make you fish food. You've cause me more trouble, and given me more loss than anyone who ever crossed me. And now you're gonna pay to ultimate price from crossing Morgan Toulair. "We'll soon be over the gulf. Just a little longer, and then, "Hello, Fish!"

As Toulair went back into the cockpit and closed the door, Gideon struggled to loosen the tape that held him.

Suddenly a hand was clapped over his mouth. Grant turned his head as far as possible and saw his friend, Sergeant Phil Early, holding his finger to his lips for Grant to remain quiet. Early quickly cut the tape from Grant's hands and feet.

Grant whispered, "How did you..."

"Later," whispered Early.

Toulair was surprised as he stepped from the cockpit. "Well, looks like I've got a stow away. More fish food."

He reached for his gun, but Early had already drawn his and when Toulair brought his pistol up to shoot Early instinctively shot him in the chest. Toulair looked surprised as he staggered against the bulkhead. He raised his gun and tried to aim it at Grant but it wavered as he pulled the trigger and the bullet went through the fuselage wall toward the wing. As he breathed his last, he asked, "Now who's gonna fly this crate?"

Chapter Forty-Nine

GRANT LOOKED AT Early and said, "That, my friend, is a very good question. And another is, How did you get on board without Toulair suspecting it?

"Against Major Jenkins advice and wishes, I made him see that was our only chance to get you out of this mess alive. I hid in a compartment I hoped Toulair would not check and it worked."

"Well, you've saved my life...for now...I think. What are we going to do when this plane runs out of gas? It's on automatic pilot for now, then what?"

Grant said, "Let's get in the cockpit and see if we can turn this thing around to head toward land."

Grant sat in the pilot's seat on the left and Early took his position in the right side.

"I guess we oughta buckle up," Gideon said. Then they looked at the bewildering array of instruments.

"I think we'll have to take it off automatic pilot to turn it," Early commented.

"Let's see if we can get anybody on the radio to tell us

what to do."

Leaving the plane on automatic pilot they both examined what they thought were the controls for the radio. Early began turning a dial that looked like it might be part of the radio and kept saying, "Hello, anybody out there?" He kept at it for over half an hour until someone responded.

"This is a UPS cargo aircraft. Who is this?"

"May day! This is a private plane on automatic pilot with a dead pilot and two guys who can't fly this thing."

"What happened to the pilot?"

"It's a long story that we don't have time for now. Can you help us turn the plane toward land?"

"What is your heading?"

"Do you mean what direction we're headed?"

"Yes. Look for it on the instrument panel."

Grant said, "It says we're going southwest."

"Okay, get a firm grip on the yoke...the steering wheel. Then turn the automatic pilot off. The aircraft will want to wander off course. You'll be flying the plane."

Phil asked, "You got all that, Gideon?"

"I think so. I've got the wheel, you turn off the autopilot."

The plane immediately started to buck and turn to the left because of the wind. Grant struggled not to panic and to keep the plane level.

The UPS pilot asked, "How'er you doin'?"

"So far so good," Grant replied. "Now what?"

"Listen closely. There are two peddles on the floor. They control the direction of flight along with the yolk. To turn the plane to the right or left, push gently on the peddle for that direction and gently turn the yolk in the same direction. It doesn't take much to turn it so be gentle with the yolk. To go up, or to slow the plane, pull the yoke back, to go down or faster push the yoke forward."

Grant grimaced and said, "All right, here goes."

Suddenly the plane jerked to the right and layed over to

the side to an alarming degree. "Whoa, too much," Grant shouted.

Keeping his foot on the right peddle and his hand on the yolk steady he brought the plane under control and finally headed in a northerly direction.

"Okay, Buddy, I've got you in sight now. You're looking pretty good. But it looks like you've got a fuel leak in the right wing."

Phil said, "That probably happened when Toulair shot at us and missed. It went through the wall in that direction."

"You've had gun fire in the plane?" the UPS pilot exclaimed.

"Yep," said Grant.

"Is that what happened to the pilot?"

"Yes, he was a fugitive from the law trying to leave the country for Mexico. I'm a private detective and my partner here is a police officer. He had abducted me and tied me to a seat. But my great friend, Phil, had stowed away in the rear of the plane and while Toulair was busy in the cockpit, he sneaked out and cut me free, just in time for Toulair to leave the cockpit and pull a gun. The rest is history."

"Are you sure he's dead?"

"Oh, yeah," Phil said. "He took a .38 right through the heart. No doubt."

The UPS pilot said, "I've been talking to air traffic control at George Bush International in Houston. Turn your radio to frequency 123.4 and you'll be able to communicate with them. They're your best bet to come out of this in one piece."

"Thank you, Sir. If you're ever up in Springfield, Missouri look us up and we'll have the best steak in town."

"Sounds like a deal. Over and out."

"Houston, do you hear us," said Phil.

"Barely, you are still pretty far out over the gulf. How much fuel do you have remaining?"

Grant said, "The left tank is empty and the right tank is

leaking from an errant gun shot."

"Yeah, the UPS pilot gave us that information. The good news is that you're headed in the right direction. The bad news is that you don't have enough fuel to get to any airport on land."

"Which means," Grant said, "we're gonna have to ride this thing down into the water."

"I don't see any other option," Houston said.

"We're going to need all the help we can get," Grant said.

"We'll do our best. Do you happen to have a life raft and or life jackets on board?"

Gideon and Phil looked at each other and shrugged. "We have no idea,"said Phil.

Grant said, "I'll keep trying to fly the plane and you go see if you can find any of that stuff."

Fifteen minutes later Phil returned and took his left seat. "No raft and only one life jacket. And I'm not much of a swimmer."

"We'll have to make do. Last winter I was dumped in the Lake of the Ozarks in freezing water and survived. At least the water will be warm."

"Houston," Grant asked, "how far from land are we now?"

"As near as we can tell, about seventy-five miles. What is your altitude, Mr. Grant?"

"If I'm reading it right, about 9,500 feet."

"Maintain your current altitude. When you run out of fuel you'll have further to glide, bringing you closer to land."

"How do we keep from coming into the water in such a way that the plane comes apart and we go down with it? Grant asked.

"That is what we need to work on while we still have time. When the engines die, push the yolk slightly forward to begin your descent. Watch your air speed, maintain air speed to 90 knots by pulling the yoke back to slow down or push the yoke forward to speed up. When you get to about 100 feet start pulling the yolk back to keep the nose up. The wind will be coming out of the west. You need to turn into the wind as you are going down if at all possible. Our goal is for you to glide on the wind and into the water without breaking up the plane."

"I wish it was as easy as it sounds," Grant lamented.

"You can do this, Grant. Just stay calm and keep thinking."

"I think it's a little late for the calm part."

"We've contacted the Coast Guard and a cutter is headed to the area where we calculate you'll come down. Keep in mind that plane is not a boat. It won't stay afloat long. Have your exit in mind and execute it as quickly as possible after you hit the water."

"Thank you, Houston…Whoops, the engines just died. Here we go!"

"Tilt the nose down so that you maintain air speed and don't stall and fall straight down. Remember to turn into the wind."

"Boy," Phil said, "this thing is really picking up speed fast."

"That's to be expected, pull the yoke back slowly." Houston said. "You're going downhill."

"What a ride," Grant said. "Silver Dollar City can't beat this."

"Read the altimeter to me," Houston said.

"We're already at 7,000 feet and going down fast," Phil said.

"Get ready to pull the nose up," Houston said.

"At 100 feet," Phil said.

Grant was struggling to keep control of the plane without power and fighting cross winds. Looking through the windshield they watched as the water of the Gulf raced toward them.

"1,000 feet," Phil shouted.

"Start pulling up the nose," Houston said. "Be easy with it. Don't jerk it."

The nose of the plane began to slowly rise. Then they felt like the plane had hit a brick wall. Water flew up on both sides of the plane, the left wing broke off causing the plane to spin around to the right. After what seemed like ten minutes, but was actually only two, the plane came to a halt, bobbing in the water. They sat there for a moment wondering how and why they were still alive.

"We're alive," shouted Phil. "Great job, Gideon."

"Yeah, but let's get out of here ASAP."

They both unbuckled their seat belts and shakily made their way out of the cockpit. Grant pulled his cell phone from his pocket and snapped a picture of Toulair's body. "I want to prove he's no longer a threat to anyone."

Looking to the rear of the aircraft he said, "There are ten deadly weapons that will never get to Mexico. Good riddance."

Sea water was pouring into the plane through the hole left by the broken left wing.

Grant helped Phil put on the life jacket and together they struggled to open the fuselage door. The water of the Gulf pushed hard against it but the adrenaline coursing through their veins gave them the extra boost needed to push it open.

"Phil," shouted Grant, "get as far from the plane as you can as quickly as you can. Otherwise, when it goes down, the suction will pull you down with it."

Together they swam away from the plane. After about fifty feet, they stopped and turned to watch it tilt forward and plunge straight down, carrying Toulair to a watery grave.

Grant, as he treaded water, said, "Now we wait. And who knows for how long."

"Hopefully, Houston can tell the Coast Guard where we

went down," Phil said.

"It's going to be dark soon," Grant said. "I hope we won't have to tread water all night. Thankfully, the swells are only about two feet."

"Put your hand on this vest. That should help you some."

After a moment Grant said, "Thanks, that does help a lot."

"We've been so busy we've forgotten to do the main thing to help," Grant said.

"What's that?"

"To pray. God is everywhere, including the Gulf of Mexico, and He is sovereign over things here, too."

"Father, Phil and I are your children. We know that you care for us and for our loved ones back home. I'm sure they are praying for us. Lord, our prayer is simple. Please help us to remain afloat until help arrives. And help the Coast Guard to find us before it's too late. Thank you for your presence and your gracious help. In Jesus Name, Amen."

And Phil responded, "Amen!"

They watched a beautiful sunset as the sun went down in the west. The waters of the Gulf became calm and smooth. The moon sent some light as they watched it and the stars appear. About an hour after sunset, the exhausted Phil Early's head rested on the life jacket and he went to sleep. Grant, with his hand on the jacket, gently kicked his feet to stay afloat as he fought to stay awake.

Using his waterproof wristwatch, he watched the hour of midnight pass. He longed for the sun rise and the arrival, hopefully, of the Coast Guard.

In the distance he thought he saw a light. As he watched he saw that it was a search light.

"Phil, wake up! I think the Coast Guard is coming."

Grant let go of the life jacket, took a deep breath, and worked to remove the white shirt he had worn to see the pastor. He held it up as high as possible while treading water hoping it would be seen by the Coast Guardsmen."

But the cutter turned the other way.

CHAPTER FIFTY

UNKNOWN TO GIDEON and Phil, there was a gathering of people in the Major Jenkins office and the hall outside his office.

"Finally," Dick Jenkins said, "I got through to the FAA. They've been in contact with air traffic control in Houston, Texas. They were in communication with Gideon and Phil when the plane went down in the Gulf. They had no idea of how bad the crash was; no idea of survivors. But the Coast Guard is searching for them. But as you know, it's dark down there, too."

"So we continue to pray," said June Whitlow, Gideon's fiancé. Tears were flowing down her cheeks. She and Beth Anne, Phil's wife, clung to each other.

June said, "Phil was so brave to go on that flight with Gideon. They've just got to be alright!"

So they waited, and cried and prayed some more.

At 2:30 a.m., Jenkins phone rang. He grabbed it quickly. "Jenkins here." He listened for a moment, held up his hand for everyone to be still. Then he shouted, "They found them! They're alive and well!

~~~~~

The cutter had circled around until a seaman, riding as high on the boat as possible shouted, “Sir, I see something off to port!”

“Hard to port,” commanded the skipper.

“When they were close enough to identify the men in the water, they launched a small rubber craft to approach and rescue them.

The guardsmen pulled the two exhausted men into their boat and quickly wrapped them in dry blankets. The air and the wind were much cooler than the warm Gulf waters.

Grant, with his teeth chattering, said, “I guess you guys know you’re an answer to a whole lot of prayers. We can’t thank you enough.”

“We’re just glad we found you. It’s hard enough in the daylight, but in the dark, it’s a miracle that we saw you.”

Aboard the cutter, Grant asked the boat commander, an ensign, if there was a way to call home.

“We’ve got a Sat-phone. Can call anywhere from anywhere. What’s the number you want to call.”

~~~~~

At 3:30 a.m., June Whitlow’s cell phone rang. The screen showed an unfamiliar number but she answered nervously, “Hello.”

“It’s me, Sweetheart. It was a close call, but with Phil’s heroic help we made it!”

“Oh, Darling, Beth Anne and I, and all the rest have been frantic not knowing what happened.”

“We’ll tell you all about it when we get home. Put Beth Anne on for Phil.”

After the phone made the rounds, it finally got to Major Jenkins. “We are all thrilled that you guys survived. How about Toulair? Did he get away?"

"Oh, no. Captain Toulair went down with the ship. He lost a gun fight with our Sergeant Phil Early."

"Can't wait to hear all about it. Sounds like I may be putting Sergeant Early up for the Medal of Valor-Silver.

CHAPTER FIFTY-ONE

LIEUTENANT CARDWELL OF the Nixa PD watched in amazement as Prosecuting Attorney Mary Matthews, her hands cuffed behind her, was led past his desk under the command of Special Agents of the FBI. Morgan Toulair's partner in crime had quickly decided that he was not going down alone.

Just as quickly, Mary Matthews, gave evidence that Toulair had engineered the death of Senator Gardner Burkes, which also led to the arrest of the two hired killers who actually did the deed.

Detective Deputy Cal Unger had the privilege of arresting Milton Sorrell and booking him into the Greene County jail. Sorrell, through his attorney, told his suspicion that Toulair had killed his friend, Bill Townsend. But of course, Toulair was now out of reach of the long arm of the law.

CHAPTER FIFTY-TWO

Saturday, July 15, 2:30 p.m.

THE AUDITORIUM OF Highland Baptist Church was packed as Gideon Grant stood trembling at the front waiting for his lovely bride, Ardith June Whitlow, to march down the aisle to meet him at the marriage altar. The months of planning had finally come to fruition. Gideon's mother, Mildred clutched her husband's arm as she turned to watch her new daughter-in-law come slowly and regally down the aisle on the arm of Major Dick Jenkins. Boyd's eyes were leaking tears of joy.

Betsy Oppermann, June's maid of honor, towered over the other ladies in the line.

In the absence of Gideon's brother, Greg, in the hospital with a broken leg suffered in a rock-climbing accident, Joe Bob Rounds stood with Gideon as best man.

Highland Baptist's new pastor, Matthew Clarkson, smiled as June arrived at the altar. *I've always loved weddings,* he thought, *never saw a bride who wasn't beautiful, and this one is especially lovely.*

"We are gathered," began the pastor, "in the sight of God and the presence of this company to join together this man, Gideon Aaron Grant, and this woman, Ardith June Whitlow in the holy bonds of matrimony…

When the ceremony was finished and the "I do's" were done, Gideon kissed June for a long time and the congregation gave them a standing ovation. They rushed from the sanctuary like someone running to a whole lot of joy.

A two-week honeymoon was planned in Oregon where Gideon had been on a previous case and couldn't wait to show June the sights. He had reserved a condo in Lincoln City on the coast where they could watch whales play and walk on the beach enjoying each other.

As they walked through a shower of rice, Gideon looked up and said, "Thank you, Jesus."

www.ingramcontent.com/pod-product-compliance
Lightning Source LLC
LaVergne TN
LVHW020043110826
845155LV00029B/623

* 9 7 8 1 9 5 1 7 7 2 8 7 1 *